The Prince of Fools

The Prince of Fools

by
Gérard de Nerval

Translated, annotated and introduced by
Brian Stableford

A Black Coat Press Book

Visit our website at www.blackcoatpress.com

ISBN 978-1-61227-872-8. First Printing: June 2019. Published by Black Coat Press, an imprint of Hollywood Comics.com, LLC, P.O. Box 17270, Encino, CA 91416. All rights reserved. Except for review purposes, no part of this book may be reproduced or transmitted in any form or by any means, electronic or mechanical, including photocopying, recording, or by any information storage and retrieval system, without permission in writing from the publisher. The stories and characters depicted in this novel are entirely fictional. Printed in the United States of America.

Introduction

Le Prince des sots, allegedly by Gérard de Nerval (Gérard Labrunie, 1808-1855), here translated as *The Prince of Fools*, was initially published as a serial in *La Nouvelle Revue* between 1 July and 15 August 1887 and reprinted in book form by Calmann-Lévy in 1888. In a preface, Louis Ulbach relates how he bought the manuscript of the novel in 1866, and concluded that it must have preceded a drama of that title that was known to have existed, thanks to the testimony of Théophile Gautier, and which had apparently adapted an episode from it (that of the Mouth of Hell). After giving a synopsis of the play, Gautier had deplored the loss of the manuscript of the play, which had presumably been destroyed.

Ulbach records that the copy of the novel he bought (he does not say from whom) had been transcribed by an awkward hand, but it was heavily overladen with corrections in Gérard de Nerval's own handwriting, with which he was familiar. He states that he kept it for twenty years without reading it, so impenetrable did it seem, but that one day, having reread Gautier's remarks on the play, he was emboldened to work on it, to salvage it and to publish what he described as "this very curious, very picturesque, very remarkable book, one of the most forceful that he wrote."

The first question one has to ask, on reading that, is: "Is it true?" Apart from Ulbach's statement, there is no other evidence that Gérard de Nerval ever wrote such a novel, and if he had, it is perhaps surprising that his close friend Théophile Gautier does not seem to have been aware of its existence, although he gave a detailed description of the play. One must therefore wonder how likely Louis Ulbach is to have perpetrated a deception of this kind, given that he would have been by no means the first writer to put another man's name of a work of his own.

Louis Ulbach (1822-1889) was one of the last survivors of the radical Romantic Movement. He edited the *Revue de Paris*, the movement's chief organ, until its suppression in 1858, in which capacity he was Gérard de Nerval's last editor prior to the latter's death. While Victor Hugo and Edgar Quinet remained in exile after being banished following Louis Napoléon's 1851 coup-d'état, and many others were muzzled by the Second Empire's censors, Ulbach carried on the struggle as best he could, often using the false signature "Ferragus" for provocative and inflammatory material, and was imprisoned more than once for his radical sentiments. He was eventually appointed as custodian of the Bibliothèque de l'Arsenal in 1878; a position once held by the great pioneer of French Romanic prose, Charles Nodier.

That Ulbach was capable of writing *Le Prince des sots*, there is no doubt, and that his character was amenable to the perpetration of such a hoax seems highly likely; as for his motivation, he was at the very end of his career in 1887, and the novel, in spite of what the preface claims, is not really finished; had it borne his own name, it would have been very difficult to publish.

On the other hand, there is no hard evidence either that Ulbach's story is not true, and the polite course of action, in consequence is to believe him. I shall therefore assume, from this point onwards, that Ulbach was telling the truth, although skeptical and cynical readers might prefer to doubt that and keep reservations in mind.

Ulbach observes that the novel was clearly written "under the influence of" Victor Hugo's *Notre-Dame de Paris—1482* (1829), and suggests that it must have been written in parallel with it, or immediately thereafter. Nerval was acquainted with Hugo while the latter was writing his classic novel—Hugo had invited Nerval to visit him and join his *cénacle* after the latter published his translation of Goethe's *Faust* in 1828—and it was through Hugo that he became fast friends with Gautier, with whom he formed the *petit cénacle* spun off from Hugo's by its younger members.

The *petit cénacle* also included two of the historians recruited to Hugo's circle: Paul Lacroix (1806-1884), alias "P. L. Jacob le bibliophile," an obsessive hunter of obscure texts, who employed his expertise in the research for several historical novels of his own, including *La Danse Macabre* (1832; tr. as *Danse Macabre*[1]), set in Paris in 1438, not long after the period in which *Le Prince des sots* is set, and which has several features in common with it, including a fascination with the hypothetical origins of theatrical performance; and Auguste Maquet (1813-1888), who did Alexandre Dumas' donkey-work for him for several years and wrote the first draft of several of his historical novels, including *Les Trois Mousquetaires* (1844). Although Maquet had not begun working for Dumas in 1831, when the latter wrote his drama, *Charles VII et ses grand vassals*—which is also set slightly later than *Le Prince des Sots* and draws on the same sources—he might have lent some assistance to it. In any case, Victor Hugo, Alexandre Dumas

---

[1] Black Coat Press, ISBN 978-1-61227-205-4.

and Paul Lacroix would all have been aware of their various works in progress, and probably exchanged comments with one another as they went along. Nerval could presumably have joined in, and perhaps he did—but if so, it is odd that Gautier, writing thirty years later, only remembered the lost drama, and not the novel on which it was apparently based.

Ulbach goes on to say in his introduction that he has done his best to make sense of the corrections the author made to the manuscript, and has "filtered" various contradictions and errors, but without changing anything or adding anything. Although he says that the novel is finished—and he regrets the fact that Nerval did not submit it to him while he was the editor of the *Revue de Paris*, so that he could work on it with him in the early 1850s, as he had on other manuscripts—it is only complete in the sense that it reaches a conclusion. The final chapter is, in effect, merely a collage of notes mapping out what was supposed to happen in the final phases of the novel, without filling in the narrative flesh. It informs the reader of what happened, but without depicting it in any detail, ignoring several problems in continuity and leaving numerous loose ends dangling, as well as some yawning gaps between the events of the novel and the known facts of history—which had been separated considerably by the impetus of the plot, perhaps to the point where the author had despaired of any possible reconciliation.

In spite of that final awkwardness, Ulbach rightly claims that the novel has much to recommend it, not only in terms of its own narrative verve and color, but perhaps in helping to fill out the picture of the early development of historical fiction within the context of the French Romantic Movement.

Maquet and Lacroix were by no means the only keen historians involved in the Movement. Gérard de Nerval's intense interest in German Romanticism was shared by Edgar Quinet (1803-1875), who had a particular interest in the philosophy of history and the long-term development of humankind, elaborately displayed in his epic novel cast in dramatic form, *Ahasuerus* (1833; tr. as *Ahasuerus*[2]). Quinet became a close friend of Jules Michelet (1798-1874) who spent much of his life writing a conspicuously Romantic narrative history of France. Augustin Thierry (1795-1856) had helped to show both of them the way, not only in his insistence on consisting original documents whenever possible but also in narrativizing the material that he took from them in the context of a political philosophy and theory of historical development.

All of the Romantic historians took considerable inspiration from Baron Montesquieu's classic *Considérations sur les causes de la grandeur des Romains et de leur décadence* (1734), which attempted to fit an account of the history of the Roman Empire into a general theory of historical change in which empires were bound by logic to follow a kind of life-cycle of rise, triumph and decay, and all of them were intensely interested in the attempt to do something similar—but necessarily more complicated—with the history of France. 1830 was a year of ostensible revolution, in which the tottering Bourbon monarchy restored after fall of Napoléon's post-Revolutionary Empire was transformed, its absolutism replaced by the constitutional monarchy of Louis-Philippe. In searching for the remote origins of the spectacular sequence of changes that had

---

[2] Black Coat Press, ISBN 978-1-61227-214-6.

been produced since the historical break of 1789, the Romantic writers of 1830 settled on the fifteenth century as the period in which the rise of a "middle class" between the nobility and the serfs—the "bourgeoisie"—had begun to sap the power of monarchy and aristocracy, leading gradually but inexorably to its inevitable fall.

It is not a coincidence that most of the writers of the French Romantic Movement were fervent Republicans, who were already looking forward to the next revolution, which would remove Louis-Philippe and put a end to monarchy once and for all. Things did not quite work out that way, and the aftermath of the 1848 Revolution, the turbulent Second Republic and the 1851 *coup-d'état* devastated the careers of all the writers cited above, and Ulbach too, sending Victor Hugo, Alexandre Dumas and Edgar Quinet into exile. Dumas accepted an amnesty from the new Emperor and returned, while Gautier, Lacroix, Gérard de Nerval and Auguste Maquet never had to leave, but they all had to work thereafter under a stern political censorship that undoubtedly stifled an important aspect of their work. Although historical fiction thrived under the Second Empire—largely because it was so difficult to publish anything set in the present day except sentimental dramas devoid of political suggestions—it had to work within vague but forceful boundaries of the acceptable.

That point is of considerable relevance to the peculiar history of *Le Prince des sots*, which could not have been published in 1831 if it was, in fact, written then, or at any time before 1848, and probably could not have been published safely between 1851 and the author's death in 1855 despite Ulbach's nostalgic regret that he had not seen it. There would have been little incentive for Gérard to try to finish it even during the brief interim of the Second Republic, when economic factors made conditions very difficult for writers. The reason why Nerval's novel, unlike Hugo's and Lacroix's novels and Dumas' play, would have a direly hazardous venture when it was allegedly written is that, although censorship was lighter under Louis-Philippe than it had been during the reigns of Louis XVIII and Charles X, it was still in force, and the censors were inevitably sensitive to overt or disguised criticisms of the king. Louis-Philippe was the Duc d'Orléans, a direct descendant of the Duc d'Orléans, also called Louis, who is the villain of *Le Prince des sots*, and is depicted therein as a despicable embodiment of all the corruptions typically consequent of not-quite-absolute power. It would have been impossible, in 1831, for anyone reading the novel not to take some critical inference from that connection.

Although the censors of the Second Empire could not have taken the particular portrayal of the villain personally, the novel's criticism of political power and its abuses is sufficiently general to have retained a certain apparent danger that would almost certainly have led to its suppression, not only while Nerval was still alive but even when Ulbach allegedly came into possession of the manuscript. Censorship had relaxed somewhat by then, but not completely, and Ulbach, considered a dangerous radial, was still being closely monitored by the censors. Nor did the fall of the Second Empire get him out of trouble; he was imprisoned under the Third Republic as well, and although he does not say a word about such difficulties in his introduction—a commentary suggestive by its conspicuous absence—Ulbach must have known that 1887 was not long after the earliest date that the novel could have been safely put into print in France.

It is worth noting in this context that, from a purely historical point of view, the author's choice of the Duc d'Orléans as his arch-villain, while a considerable sympathy is extended to his great rival, the son of the Duc de Boulogne, who became known as Jean *Sans Peur* [John the Fearless] was largely arbitrary. It is true that some of the chronicles Nerval used as sources suggest that Orléans might have been the lover of the queen during the alleged madness of Charles VI, but there is no evidence beyond mere rumor. It has to be remembered that all history is propaganda and that slander is always its most effective weapon. Perhaps Orléans really was an exceptionally cruel *débauché*, and he certainly helped his fellow noblemen to oppress and exploit the emergent bourgeoisie in order to support the luxury of their lifestyle, but there is no real evidence that he was any worse than his peers, or that his arch-enemy was any better. Melodrama, however, requires contrast and contest, and historical melodrama requires virtue and heroism in order to manufacture and sustain its underlying narrative of progress.

Since the time of its publication, of course, *Le Prince des sots* has come to seem quite anodyne in political terms. If elements of its criticism of the routine abuse of power still retain a certain relevance, it is in the context of a continuing storm of protest that is nowadays almost impossible to suppress and difficult even to inhibit. That is, however, not the only aspect of the novel that would have been interesting had it seen the light of day in 1831 or 1866, and its central character is not its villain's rival, but an ambiguous individual whose heroism, if it is heroism, has a very different character, and one who clearly does not belong to the period in which the novel is set: the *Prince des sots*. That title does not appear to have been used in France for at least hundred years after the period in which the novel is set, and it was then applied to the French equivalent of the English "Lord of Misrule," who was granted a temporary "royalty" in English courts on one day of the year—usually Christmas—in which the traditional order was notionally overturned and the aristocracy put on a show of surrendering their authority briefly to their servants.

Nerval's *prince des sots* is a lord of misrule of sorts, but a subtle one, a primitive anarchist undermining the aristocratic order invisibly and subtly, through the medium of entertainment. His activities are similar in some respects to those of the sinister Macabre, the supposed inventor of the *danse macabre* in Paul Lacroix's novel, and the character also echoes a key scene in *Notre-Dame de Paris—1482*, in which poor Quasimodo is elected to a role similar to that of the Lord of Misrule in a "Festival of Fools." All three works project into an obscure past the hypothetical origins of modern theater, in order to built an argument regarding a subversive role played by theatrical performance in social progress—an argument inevitably dear to the hearts of the French Romantics, who saw the première of Hugo's *Hernani* in 1831 as a revolution of sorts, to which the members of the *petit cénacle* were requested by the author to serve as mercenaries, ready for a pitched battle if one should prove necessary. The members of the *cénacles* saw themselves as the jesters of their era—*Enfants sans souci* [Carefree Children] as Nerval names Gonin's troupe—pursuing an essentially subversive quest in a deliberately preserve manner. How effective they were in that role it is difficult to assess, but they certainly persuaded the forces opposing them that they might be, sufficiently to attract active suppression and even a certain modest martyr-dom.

Having made that point, however, it must be admitted that of the many loose ends that are not tied up in the synoptic final chapter of the novel, perhaps the most introducing is that of the *prince des sots*' motivation. He lends himself to various projects of the rich and powerful in the interests of his own survival, but the way he goes about fulfilling his various missions is very peculiar, routinely featuring showmanship for the sake of showmanship and subversion for the sake of subversion. In that, he surely resembles many writers of the Romantic Movement more than a little, perhaps Gérard de Nerval and Louis Ulbach most of all. Although Nerval was not the only member of the group who cultivated a reputation for periodic mental illness, and not the only one who died in strange circumstances, an apparent suicide,[3] he was certainly the most extreme, and he took his role very seriously, even though he probably never made up his own mind as to exactly what his motivation was or ought to be. The novel reflects that uncertainty, and was perhaps part and parcel of the author's attempt to work through it. If so, the fact that its ending is tokenistic, and that the novel itself was apparently lost or cunningly disguised, might take on an extra significance and measure of intrigue.

---

[3] Gérard de Nerval was found hanged from the bar of a cellar window in a dingy back-street in January 1855. Baudelaire suggested that it was a statement of sorts that Gérard had "delivered his soul in the darkest street he could find."

This translation was made from the version of the Calman-Lévy edition reproduced on the Bibliothèque Nationale's *gallica* website.

Brian Stableford

I. THE COURT OF AMOUR

The crowd filled the bright room
Amid vapors scented with sandalwood,
The monarch was enthroned. Beside him, benevolent,
The queen had the splendor of the nascent moon,
And the Fool the gaze of a triumphant buffoon.

It is known that the French kings of the first two dynasties, the Merovingians and the Carolingians, never lived in Paris, and that it was the Capetians who first resided there, having chosen the edifice now called the Palais de Justice.

It is also known that Charles V, of the Valois dynasty, having a horror of that palace, in which he had suffered various outages during the troubles provoked by Marcel, abandoned it in order to go and live in a house of pleasure built near the Église Saint-Pol, from which it took its name. He had a fortress constructed not far away in order to contain his treasures, the Bastille, inaugurated as a state prison by the provost Hugues Aubriot, who had helped to build it.[4]

---

[4] Charles V of France (1338-1380)—not to be confused with the Holy Roman Emperor Charles V, usually known as Charles Quint—succeeded to the throne in 1364. He contrived to turn the tide temporarily in the Hundred Years War and reclaim a great deal of territory from the English. Étienne Marcel, the provost of the merchants of Paris, had been a thorn in the side of his predecessor, Jean II, forcing many reforms that weakened royal power, and maintaining an opposition that helped to prompt the peasant revolt of the derisively nicknamed "Jacquerie" in 1358, which was crushed by Charles II

It is in the Hôtel Saint-Pol, which had vast gardens surrounded by walls, able if necessary to withstand a siege, that the scenes of this study occur, which only seems to be a novel, because it is a true history.

At the end of the fourteenth century there were no paved streets, drains or street lights. The houses were absolutely lacking in comfort; the only items of furniture princely dwellings possessed were a few chairs and a dresser serving simultaneously as a writing desk, a cupboard and a bed.

The Hôtel Saint-Pol was an exception. However, a simple curtain of blue serge decorated the walls of the great hall where the Court of Amour was held, presided over by Isabeau de Bavière, where a quantity of young women assembled, mingled with faces more or less bearded.[5]

A strange thickset individual, who was neither handsome nor ugly, with the vivacity of a monkey, agitated in that noble assembly. Of all those who had seen him or had talked to him, none could say: "He has this

---

of Navarre. Charles VI (1368-1422) was only twelve when he succeeded his father, and the brief Regency of his uncles undid much of the good work that Charles V had done in restoring the financial stability of the realm.

[5] The original *cours d'amour* [courts of amour] were a twelfth-century invention that flourished in the south of France under the influence of Aliénor d'Aquitaine and Marie de Champagne. The imitation featured in the story was actually instituted in 1401 on the initiative of Duc Louis II de Bourbon (one of the uncles of Charles VI given a minor in the present story) and Philippe de Bourgogne. The usage here is therefore anachronistic, as the key events described in the early chapters occurred in 1393, but not as anachronistic as the introduction of the Prince of Fools.

appearance, or this accent," so much did he vary his pose, his gestures and his voice. He was the Prince of Fools.

In the middle of the hemicycle where the platform occupied by the queen stood there was a young woman, pretty in her modest appearance, like a Phyllis or a Chloe of the sheepfold. She wore the simple costume of the daughters of the people, but with what grace! And abundant ebony black hair imprisoned in a steel ring framed her charming face, crimson with modesty.

"Come, my dear, advance and state your complaint," said Isabeau de Bavière, who was seated next to her royal spouse.[6] "Speak without fear. Our court of amour will give you good and loyal justice if, as we hope, you have right on your side."

"Alas, Madame la Reine," the young woman replied, lowering her eyes, "I have a great sadness in my heart and also a great shame..."

"Be reassured," said Isabeau. "First, tell us who you are."

"Coline Demerre, daughter of the barber of the marketplace."

"How old are you?"

"Sixteen years."

"Good. Now tell us what brings you before us."

---

[6] Isabeau de Bavière [Isabeau of Bavaria] (c.1370-1435) married Charles VI in 1385; she gave birth to twelve children, four of whom died young; Charles VII was the eleventh. Two of Isabeau's daughters married kings of England; Isabella married Richard II before marrying Charles, Duc d'Orléans (the son of the one featured in the story); and Catherine married Henry V after Agincourt, before marrying Owen Tudor, the progenitor of the Tudor dynasty.

"I have followed the straight path for sixteen years," said Coline, her eyes lowered.

The Prince of Fools whispered some quip in the ear of Sire Hugues de Guisay regarding the months of nursing passed without stumbling, with excited the hilarity of the gentleman.

"Sire Hugues," exclaimed Charles VI, severely, "Our court of amour is a serious tribunal; please remember that. We have revived this ancient institution in order to bring a remedy to debauchery, which, under the cover of gallantry, threatens to invade everything."

Then, addressing all the lords, the king added: "Be careful, Messieurs; constant amour has become a subject of ridicule; the faith of the ancient knights is considered as an obsolete fashion. But where are the valor and honor of old? All that holds firm."

While Charles VI was speaking, the men affected a bleak silence, but a smile of approval was designed on the lips of the ladies.

"Coline Demerre," said Isabeau, "continue your story."

"I had entered into the service of Madame de Bourbon," said Coline. "Now, a great lord who often visits Madame la Duchesse cast his eyes upon me...."

"And he made you quit the straight path?" the king interjected.

"How could a poor girl like me rest the seductions of..."

"Go on," said the queen, in an imperative voice.

"Monseigneur le Duc d'Orléans."

"Orléans!" murmured Isabeau, quivering.

"My brother!" the king exhaled, in a sigh.

"Who has enabled you to dare to attack such a highly-placed person?" cried the queen, darting a gaze flamboyant with hatred at Coline.

"God is my witness, Madame, that the Duc has done what I accuse him of having done."

"Where is the Duc?" Isabeau demanded, sharply, of Hugues de Guisay.

"Monseigneur is witnessing the marriage of one of his officers."

"I regret that he is not present to confound the audacity of this girl."

"Perhaps he would be very embarrassed."

"Do you think that she is telling the truth?"

"I think, Madame, pardon the great liberty, that the Duc might well have been able to forget..."

"And you, Sire Hugues," the queen interrupted, "are forgetting the respect that you owe him."

"Dear Isabelle," said the king, interrupting, "such grand words are out of place. Remember why the court of amour has been instituted. Is it not to judge cases of this sort? What does quality matter? A prince of the blood, like a simple bourgeois, is answerable to this tribunal. I don't intend to condemn my brother without hearing him. Let's postpone the case to our next session."

"Let it be as you desire," said Isabeau, "but before retiring, I still have one question to ask the plaintiff. Do you know, my dear," she continued, with a feigned mildness, "for whom the Duc quit you?"

"Only too well, Madame la Reine," replied Coline, sighing. "It is for a noble demoiselle of the city of Orléans, whose name is Mariette d'Anghuien."

At that name, Sire Hugues started laughing madly. "By all the unicorns of the blazon!" he exclaimed.

"That's today's groom well favored, for the bride is Mariette d'Anghuien."

"All is repaired on that side," said the king. "It will be the same for you, my dear," he added, turning to Coline, "if your testimony is confirmed. Our court of amour was not instituted for any other end. My brother will find you a husband among his men-at-arms."

"As proper as the husband of Mariette d'Anghuien to play the role of Menelaus," quipped Sire Hugues, "as in your farce of the destruction of Troy, Prince of Fools."

"That one," riposted Master Gonin, the Prince of Fools, "has all the right color, with the red hair and the drooping shoulders. He'll play Saint Joseph delightfully in the mystery of the conception with the teeth-gnashers or the imprudents drawn from the Court of Miracles."[7]

The queen, who had only lent a distracted ear to that dialogue, emerged from her reverie to announce that she was ending the session.

"A moment's respite, if you'll permit, Madame," said Hugues. "I have a proposition to submit to you."

"Speak," said Isabeau

"What I have to ask of Your Majesty enters perfectly into the attributions of courts of amour. To be convinced of that, one only has to consult the archives of all those of the provinces of Puy, Aix, Avignon, Marseille, Toulouse... They have arrogated a right of ratification over incongruous marriages, such as a widower with a

---

[7] The term *Cour des miracles* [Court of Miracles] became an argot term for the poorest quarters of France in the sixteenth and seventeenth centuries; the one featured extravagantly and fancifully in Victor Hugo's *Notre-Dame de Paris—1482* is probably anachronistic.

widow, an old man with a virgin, a novice with a debauchee…now, that last case is that of today."

"And what an excellent subject of mummery at this carnival time!" cried Master Gonin.[8]

"Hey, Messire non-imprudent teeth-gnasher," said Charles VI, "calm your fervor. I'm weary of seeing my écus and my florins dissipated in decorations, costumes and music; my gold coin is turning into monkey money…"

"Think, Sire, that for such a spectacle a cortege of fans and satyrs would suffice for accessories; as for the principal role, it would only cost the trouble of extracting from a cupboard the costume of the horned bishop, who would never appear at such a fête.

"A fine figure the husband would make," said Hugues, "with the crosier and the miter with ran's hors. That would lend itself to laughter throughout Lent."

"And do you think that Monsieur d'Orléans would laugh at a farce played with his intention? What do you think, Isabeau? You're very thoughtful, Madame!"

"I'm listening. Yes, it would be a delightful fête: the lady, the husband and the lover. What a fortunate idea, fortunate and moral! The court of amour could do no better to punish the seducer."

The king, struck by that last observation, which did, indeed punish with public criticism, and attributing Isabeau's irony to the indignation of the president, only made one objection: "What about the Duc?"

---

[8] The ball at which Charles VI narrowly escaped death actually took place on 29 January 1393, not during the pre-Lent carnival; the event was organized by the queen to celebrate the wedding of one of her maids of honor.

"The Duc has too much wit to be annoyed by a malice of the Prince of Fools."

"As you think that Louis won't be annoyed, I yield, and I'll play a role. We might as well take some joyous leisure now that the realm is tranquil, thanks to the truce we've concluded with England. So, Master Gonin, chief of the Carefree Children, come and regulate a point of the ceremonial of the fête, which concerns us. We intend to involve ourselves with it, in a pleasant and mythological costume, which will render us unrecognizable to anyone not of our company. In that regard, Messeigneurs, we intend that the scene that occurred two years ago, at the baptism of the dauphin, will not be repeated. It was a very bad mummery to extinguish all the lights; the honor of the ladies received some affliction, Master Fool, make sure that nothing is lacking the fête while you are there, and to our treasury when you are there no longer.

The Prince of Fools bowed, and at the same time he raised his voice, so as to make it mocking: "That's a play on words of your grace, Sire, an antithesis, as we said in rhetoric in my day at the college in Cut-Throat Street. Oh, good times—we had an old professor there..."

"Good, good, let's not change the thesis. The provost of our palace has complained may a time that several items of our tableware disappear on days when your troupe comes to organize our fêtes."

"Faith of a man, Sire, the provost is an old thief who ought to be hanged. It's him who has stolen those items. I'll give you proof of it tomorrow, begging you, if it's clear and precise, to grant the charge of King of

Ribauds to my cousin, for whom I can answer as for myself."[9]

"All right! But keep watch on your fools."

The Prince of Fools bowed again and drew way precipitately, for fear of that the order might be countermanded. Charles VI, a sickly king who had surges of health, only to fall back into alarming melancholy and dejection, often repented an hour later of having yielded an hour before to one of Isabeau's ruinous fantasies.

In his precipitation, the chief of the Carefree Children bumped into a lord who was entering at that moment, and stood aside, shrinking and apologizing to Jean, Duc de Nevers, the heir to the duchy of Bourgogne, one of the great vassals of the crown; but the Duc interrupted him in a jovial voice.

"From prince to prince there's only a hand; take this one, Grand Duc!"

And, seizing Master Gonin's hand, he shook it amicably in his own, which was strong enough and large enough to serve as a vice if necessary.

In fact, that square-shouldered prince with a neck like a bull, a fulgurant physiognomy, and legs that were slightly twisted but muscular and wiry, was the type-specimen of those robust knights circled with steel inside in order to wear iron outside, the caryatids of the Middle Ages.

---

[9] The modern meaning of *ribaud* is "débauché," but an armed corps known as the Ribauds was founded in Paris in 1189 by Philippe-Auguste, whose leader was known as the *roi des ribauds* [king of the ribauds]. The militia was suppressed by Philippe the Bel but resurrected later in the fourteenth century with a more limited role, more akin to a police force.

He approached the king, who did not perceive him immediately, and murmured in his ear: "Sire, there are thieves in your court more to be feared than the Carefree Children."

"Ha ha! How long have you been there, cousin Bourgogne?"

"A few moments; I was told that you were holding council, and I have to talk to the king about political matters."

"Oh, very well," said the king, yawning. "But who said anything to you about thieves?"

"I'm alluding to your uncles," replied the churl, boldly, "Anjou, Berry and Bourbon."

"Bah! That's an old story," sighed the king, shrugging his shoulders. "You're belated... but since you want to talk politics, we'll render to the grand council and give you an audience."

Then the king, saluting the ladies after having kissed the queen's hand, ordered the lords to follow him and went out on the arm of Jean de Nevers.

As soon as the king and a dozen gentlemen had drawn away, the court of amour disintegrated. Each lady approached her friend's seat; groups formed and private conversations, as quiet as a swarm of bees collecting pollen, hummed beneath the paneling of the hall. All the young and noble chatelaines, taking their embroidery from their baskets, found occupation for their fingers. Their lips embroidered commentaries on the concluded audience of the court of amour.

The pensive queen had withdrawn, frowning, her mouth taut.

A painter was lacking for the charming scene if that gathering. A few formed a circle around the immense fireplace, where half a tree-trunk was being consumed, crackling.

Christine de Pisan, leaning against the wood of her stall, seemed to be paying attention to the speech fluttering around her, but the beautiful Venetian was doubtless thinking about the moral dicta that she was planning to write.[10] Next to her, the young wife of the chamberlain Savoisy, majestic in her bearing, was winding golden thread around a little nacre bobbin. Further away, one of Isabeau de Bavière's maids of honor, with a delicate complexion and blonde hair, was reciting a ballad by Alain Chartier to herself in a soft voice.[11] The lively Maréchale de Boucicault was making noisy exclamations, reading everything and nothing, and pricking her neighbors with her silver needle.[12]

---

[10] *Le Livre de la cité des dames* (c.1405; tr. as *The Book of the City of Ladies*), an early classic of feminism, written in opposition to the enormously popular *Roman de la rose. Le Trésor de la cité des dames* is a companion work, a treatise on the education of women written at about the same time. Christine de Pisan or Pizan (1364-c.1430), a protégé of Louis, Duc d'Orléans (1372-1407), was one of Charles VI's court scribes, and became an enormously important writer and publisher in the early days of the fifteenth century; her *Livre de la Paix* (1413) is a pioneering work of pacifism, and her rapid poetic celebration of Jeanne d'Arc's military victory in 1429 provided the foundation-stone of the literary legend.

[11] The presence of the poet Alain Chartier (1385-1430) at this point in the story is anachronistic; his earliest known poem dates from 1416.

[12] The wife of Jean II Le Meingre, Maréchal Boucicault was Antoinette de Turenne (1380-1416). They were married in 1393, after the ball featured in the story, but that anachronism is slight.

Among the ladies, of various ages, the Duchesse de Berry, a beautiful blonde, could be distinguished, along with Madame d'Anjou, no less blonde and no less becoming, and the Princesse de Bourbon, grave and serious, as if the session of the court of amour had not been lifted. She was illuminating precious vellum, while her daughter, an adorable she-devil of thirteen or fourteen, was running after a charming greyhound that was gamboling madly through the groups.

In order to leave the field free for those noisy frolics, the groups broke up and the ladies gathered together. Was it not necessary to talk, after the matter of the amours of the Duc d'Orléans, about the famous masquerade? It was high time to think about a costume. The embroideries went back into the baskets and the entire swarm flew away in order to take the samite coats and the hennins from the dressers and make sure that they were worthy to dress and coiff such beautiful and great ladies.

II. THE COUNCIL OF STATE

We have seen the people and the court face to face,
The armored nobility in brilliant squadrons.
The knights, in the cruel iron, rushing to slaughter;
The courtiers, trembling and vile with their armories,
The people, sublime in their rags.

The sun was declining when the king and the Duc de Nevers, followed by the members of the Council of State, penetrated beneath the vault decorated with arabesques. The light, traversing windows with his arched casements, played over rich drapes laminated with gold and silver and French fleurs-de-lys, which covered the walls of the grand council chamber.

In the center stood a long, broad table, ornamented by a green serge cloth with red tassels. In the middle of the cloth was a large rose embroidered in white wool, supporting a monstrous ink-well containing sand, sealing-wax and the royal seal. Papers and pens were scattered around it.

Seated facing one another were Charles VI and Alain Chartier, his secretary,[13] ready to write to the sovereign's dictation.

After each member of the council had taken his place, head bared, while the king alone retained his hood, Charles VI said to Jean de Nevers, who had remained standing, as was customary when one wanted to speak: "See, my cousin, how rapidly our court of amour has been transformed into a council of state. Often, it's

---

[13] Charles VI's secretary in 1393 was actually Pierre Salmon.

no less important—amour gives rise to as many concerns as hatred. But you wanted to talk to us about a serious matter. Speak."

"No one is unaware, Sire, that Sigismund of Hungary,[14] your feudal ally, is about to see his realm invaded by Turks if Christian kings do not bring him assistance. More than once he has already summoned you to his aid, and I have come to remind you of it, for there is such a racket of celebrations and feasts around you that the voice of a friend in dire straits risks not being heard."

Those proud words troubled the king. "Jean de Nevers, is it really you who is raising such a big question, you who have not yet take part in our councils?"

The young man was about to respond but he was distracted by the arrival of Louis d'Orléans, whom he suddenly perceived at the back of the hall, stopping on the threshold and giving orders to his page, whom he sent away as soon as he saw Jean de Nevers.

Instinctively, Duc Jean divined that he was no stranger to the words exchanged between the prince and the page. He went violently red, and then constrained himself.

"It s true, sire, that I have not yet taken part in your councils. However, I see here someone who is scarcely my elder but who mingles in ruling the state, as old men experienced and savant in political science may do."

---

[14] The Holy Roman Emperor Sigismund (1368-1437) became King of Hungary in 1387. In 1396 he led the combined armies of Christendom—including a large French contingent led by the son of Philippe de Bourgogne, nicknamed Jean *Sans Peur* [Jean the Fearless] (1371-1419)—against the Turks, in the so-called Crusade of Nicopolis; it was a disaster, the Christian forces being devastated under the walls of Nicopolis.

"Good God, Monsieur, do you dare to make allusion to our person?"

"Heaven forbid! King you are and you follow your métier of king legitimately." Standing aside in order to unmask his advancing antipathy, he pointed at the Duc d'Orléans, adding: "It's a matter of my cousin there."

The physiognomy of Charles VI, darkened momentarily, became expansive and radiant as soon as he perceived his brother, and welcomed him with a smile. "Aha! You've returned, Louis. Take your place. We have many things to discuss. But first, let us occupy ourselves with responding to the Duc de Nevers."

"If you'll permit, brother, I'll take charge of that."

An affirmative nod of the head encouraged the Duc d'Orléans.

"Is our cousin weary of the métier of war, in which he had already acquired so much renown?" he said "Does he believe that he has accomplished enough labors to repose in the Council of State?"

"Your presence here, handsome cousin..."

Jean de Nevers emphasized the word handsome. He was interrupted by Louis d'Orléans, who, laughing superbly and drawing himself up to his full height said: "Go on! I accept the epithet handsome, which is a grace of royal blood. Enough others ornament the other side of the coin."

Nevers bit his lip, and all the members of the council creased the corners of their mouths, unable to do more or less. In fact, the Duc d'Orléans was very handsome, very well-made, very gracious and very amiable. He was the type-specimen of a noble and gallant knight, irreproachably dressed and very luxurious.

The Duc de Nevers went on: "Your presence here, handsome cousin, can scarcely make me think that military labors are the obligatory prelude to political life."

The king intervened, and cut short that peevish persiflage.

"Messieurs, are we gathered in this place to hear you contest in bitterness and bad jokes, as you always do? Let's return to the remonstration addressed to us but our cousin Bourgogne on the subject of the delay we are bringing to aiding Sigismund of Hungary."

"That remonstration, Sire, since it pleases you to call it that, is not made by the Duc de Nevers; it emanates from Philippe de Bourgogne, The words of the son are the echo of the sentiments of the father."

"Well," riposted Orléans, like a crossbow bolt, "let the same echo report this faithfully. We are good God-fearing Christians, but the time of the crusades is past and will not be reborn. France is at peace for the first time, since the regency of our three uncles has given way to the government of our brother, the king..."

So saying, Louis de France designated with his eyes the three Ducs d'Anjou, de Berry and de Bourbon, who did not flinch.

Orléans went on: "Now, two wounds by which the fatherland lost all its blood, one toward England and the other toward Italy, are scarcely closed; the slightest movement might reopen them and render them more painful. We have done everything for peace and we hope to conserve it; it will return France to a prosperous condition. The lily, the emblem of our monarchy, cannot flourish in the midst of tempests."

"That emblem is deceptive and degenerate," relied Jean de Nevers. "The old kings of France bore in their armories not *fleurs-de-lys* but *fers-de-lance*; that was to inform them that monarchy can only be maintained and increase in strength by means of war. They certainly understood that well, the kings your ancestors, Sire, in organizing a perpetual war in Palestine that maintained the valor of the French lords, calling a truce to their discords and purging the land of the excess of the turbulent population that has so frequently troubled the throne since… and look at where we are! We have peace, in fact, but where do you see prosperity? Enemies are no longer ravaging our provinces, but it is your nobles who are insulting and pillaging the people, and after them their varlets, and after their varlets their packs, to the extent that nothing remains. It is no longer the expenses of war that are exhausting the coffers of the State, it is the expenses of luxury, of fêtes! Add to that fact that the conduct in question is increasingly destroying the affection of the population for the monarchy and their respect for the nobility. How many rebellions have already given you that advice? You have seen taxes refused, great cities like Paris and Rouen withdrawing from royal authority; the Jacques and the Maillotins[15] have proved that the villeins no longer dread your great ironclad horses and the blazoned armor of your knights, Many a time you have had them try on your harness to see whether they were of a stature, and with visors lowered, nothing any longer distinguished the vassal from the lord. What rem-

---

[15] The "Maillotin revolt" against fiscal oppression occurred in 1382, not long after Charles VI inherited the throne, when his three uncles took advantage of their regency to enrich themselves. The king, then aged fourteen, was on campaign in Flanders at the time, but his troops suppressed the revolt after his return to Paris, which he was allowed to enter without resistance.

edy is there for all that? War, I have said, a generous and holy war, in which the nobility will revivify its almost-effaced armories in the blood of infidels and will recover its lost but ever-due consideration in the eyes of the populace!"

That speech produced a great sensation, but Orléans restored equilibrium.

"The consideration of the populace? That's fine talk! Do those stupid people dare to judge the lords and masters that God has given them? What good are they, except to work like beasts of burden without other wages? Are they made for us or are we made for them? Oh, the vile people, ugly and dirty, who bark and bite like a dog, with no more discernment. Good God! Since our war in Flanders, I hate them, and above all those of Paris, the equal of vicious animals. Did the principal cities of France not say public prayers against us in favor of the rebels we were going to fight? And on our return, what did we find? The Parisian rabble had taken control of the government, and if the frightened bourgeois had not opened the gates to us, it would have been necessary to lay siege of Paris. And it's in such a state of affairs that the nobility ought to go and get themselves killed four hundred leagues from here, leaving their property and power to the Maillotins, to the Jacques, or to any other popular party? In honor, I'd rather see France in the power..."

"Brother!" cried Charles VI, standing up. "Return to the question, don't blaspheme; who will proclaim 'Vive la France!' if not Louis de France?"

The king having sat down, a murmur of approval appeased him. Jean de Nevers smiled.

The Duc d'Orléans apologized, and added: "As for our luxury, our fêtes and our profusions, which you crit-

34

icize, son of Philippe, they serve our politics more than our pleasures. It is necessary to keep in its poverty the people who raise their heads as soon as they are no longer wretched, and profit from our lack of money to redeem themselves from servitude, with the consequence that half the country will soon find itself free, a condition that in such people is monstrous and against nature."

At the sign of negation that Bourgogne made, Sire Hugues de Guisay, approving the politics of the king's brother, supported him.

"Outside of the cities," he said, "the majority of which are free now, do we not see in the country peasants who have their own houses, their own lands, their own farms..."

"Have I not said it? It's monstrous," cried Orléans, looking at his cousin ironically, "while so many nobles believe that they have their wives to themselves!"

Jean de Nevers did not appear moved by that thrust in the heart; he only murmured, so quietly that no one heard: "Poor Marguerite."

"There are some," said Sire Hugues, "who ride horses, as gentlemen do, who are followed by varlets, as our varlets are by packs of hounds."

Every member of the council, following the example of the Seigneur de Guisay, put in his word, his derisory abuse.

"You're going too far in your speech, Messieurs," observed the king, with a mixture of nervous impatience and benevolence. "I truly don't see any harm in the populace enjoying some ease and some liberty. It's a fault of general education that I recognize today, to have taken too little account of people of low estate, who sometimes don't lack courage or nobility of soul; so I don't think, like our brother, that it's necessary to overwhelm them with charges and taxes with the sole aim of keeping them in submission. I've abolished several taxes, at the request of the Chancellor of the University, and I shall abolish more, in due course. I oppose as much as I can the dilapidation of the public purse. But as for our frequent fêtes, of which you complain, Jean de Bourgogne, it's my poor health that it's necessary to reproach for them. The physicians repeat to me incessantly that I can only be cured by means of distractions and pleasures."

"Sire, your health does not seem so poor..."

"It's better, doubtless, but you're forgetting that the black thoughts and failures of intellect to which I'm inclined were caused by the fatigues of a warrior expedition; a shock would be sufficient to renew them, perhaps to make them worse. However, although it isn't permissible for me to go, like the kings my ancestors, to combat the infidels, for God and for honor, I can send aid—not very considerable, it's true, because of the ill-assured state of things, but to which I believe I can give great importance in the eyes of our ally by putting you in charge of it, Duc de Nevers.

"You fill me with joy and pride, Sire."

The king made a sign to the Maréchal de France, Jean de Boucicault, his childhood friend, to approach him. They conversed together for a few minutes in low voices. When the Maréchal returned to his seat, Alain Chartier, having drawn up a sort of official account of the session, passed it to Charles VI, who signed it and immediately handed it to the chamberlain, Charles de Savoisy.[16] Then he spoke again.

---

[16] Charles de Savoisy, Baron de Seignelay (1368-1420) was a childhood friend of Charles VI; he became his chamberlain in 1388, but became closely linked with the Duc d'Orléans after

"You can see, cousin Bourgogne," the king said, "that the session has fatigued me...my head is weak. Return tomorrow at the hour of the council; we'll occupy ourselves in regulating all this. If, in the meantime, you wish to take part in our fête this evening, it will be noisy and joyful...I need brightness, gaiety and dancing. It distracts me, elevates me from the melancholy that has, it appears, threatened me reason..."

"God protect you, Sire, and France too."

"Thank you for the king, my brother, Duc de Nevers," said the Duc d'Orléans. "Oh, if you come this evening, bring us Madame Marguerite de Hainaut.[17] She will shine in the court no less than Madame Venus in Olympus, and it will be a great honor for you, her fortunate husband."

"Her Vulcan, to follow the allegory," muttered Sire Hugues.

"Thank you, cousin d'Orléans, but Madame Marguerite would be out of place at your fêtes and mummeries. The ladies of your court are better dressed, more brilliant. She would feel very embarrassed. Thank you, I say, and adieu."

With that general salutation, Bourgogne left the hall, which did not take long to be deserted by its commensals, the session having ended. Soon, only the two brothers remained together.

---

the king's madness, and had a very checkered career thereafter. He is the leading character in Alexandre Dumas' 1831 drama *Charles VII chez ses grand vassaux*.

[17] The character called Marguerite de Hainaut here is more usually known as Marguerite de Bavière (1363-1424). She married Jean de Nevers in 1385 and gave birth to eight children.

"It's an excellent idea, Sire, to send that dull Bourguignian away from the court. He displeases me greatly with his censorial tone and his cattle-trader's costume. The entire Bourgogne family reeks of the people, as if it emerged therefrom."

"He is, however, a fine knight; I esteem him more than I like him…"

While chatting thus, the two brothers drew away from the session hall and went through the galleries of the Hôtel Saint-Pol leading to the garden, when they traversed. They went up the steps of the perron of the other wing of the edifice, where the apartments inhabited by the king were located, and went into one of the rooms, with a vast fireplace, the hearth of which, furnished with an enormous blazing log fore, was spreading a mild and warm heat, although it was necessary to sit down next to it to feel all of its force.

The two princes drew closer together, each taking a seat and remaining there momentarily, warming themselves.

At that moment the shadow of a woman was designed on the back wall, which was not covered with tapestry but with coarse Flanders leather, against which a few paintings were hung, by Jehan Muret, the Titian of the epoch, the professor of Louis d'Orléans, who had taught him to paint on glass.[18]

After a slight shiver, Charles VI raised the delicate question of Coline Demerre, seduced and abandoned, to pass on to that of the marriage of Mariette d'Anghuien, asking the name of the officer who as lending a jovial hand to the caprices of a prince possessed of a young and pretty wife, as the lovely Valentine Visconti was,

---

[18] This character is fictitious.

neglected by her lord and master in the depths of her Hôtel de Brehaigne.[19]

It was a lecture on morality that the elder brother was about to give the younger, when Queen Isabeau de Bavière appeared and placed herself between the two brothers, but at a distance, examining both, comparing the one, gracious and well-built, with the king, so frail, sickly, pale-faced, with undistinguished features, and not making use of the sagacity with which Heaven had endowed him.

Isabeau felt a scornful pity for that chilly, shivering spouse, forgetting that the Hôtel Saint-Pol was poorly heated, and that, the council chamber having no fireplace, the king had got cold there. It was a frequent accident, even at court.

Historical documents reveal that the halls where the Parlement sat, at even o'clock in the morning, were only illuminated by two candles of yellow wax and that no fire was ever lit there. The magistrates were so cold that audiences were often suspended,

In the Hôtel Saint-Pol, the chronicle says, there were three fires, in the king's bedroom, the queen's bedroom and the room where we are at present. It was out of consideration for the ladies that a faggot was lighted in the hall of the court of amour when it was in session; it was extinguished immediately afterwards, if it was not consumed entirely.

---

[19] Valentine Visconti (1371-1408), who married the Duc d'Orléans in 1389, cannot have been entirely neglected, as she gave birth to eight children, although four died in infancy, but she was exiled from the court and from Paris in the late 1390s, allegedly because of the queen's enmity.

III. ISABEAU DE BAVIÈRE

Often a frightful dream arrests my sleep,
Weighs upon my breast and hastens my awakening;
Ambition, desires, amour and jealousy
Snatch my instants and divide my life.

Alert, proud and imperious, with inadmissible frowns that spread from the corners of her lips, Isabeau de Bavière seemed at first to be violent and malevolent, but the habitual state of her physiognomy presented the slightly severe placidity of Germanic beauties. Gallic blood, mixed with Scandinavian blood and Italian blood, blossomed in a splendid drabness. Her face was half-oval, with a slightly aquiline nose, thin lips, emphatically arched and well-furnished eyebrows, large blue eyes shaded by long silky lashes, the irises of which shone in a voluptuous mist, and rosy and white cheeks. She had plump, dainty hands, admirably contoured. Her relaxed bearing was more meridional than occidental, partaking of a voluptuous abandonment and a languid grace.

She was cheerful, jovial, sometimes frolicsome, but not at the moment, when the sculptural gravity of the body combined with the low brow of the face, and the lips pale with chagrin, to enable her feline charm easily to become a leonine fascination.

Not having been perceived by the two brothers, Isabeau hesitated as to whether to approach or to draw away as silently as she had come. Should she wait for an opportunity for an encounter without a witness, to be alone with Monseigneur d'Orléans?

A residue of modesty combated in the wife against the effervescence of the lover, disdaining any restraint. Modesty struggled in vain against jealousy; passion prevailed, the statue glided over the paving stones and found herself facing the prince, who immediately stood up in order to offer her his seat, saying: "What, Madame! It's you? What a fortunate surprise!"

"You ought to be ashamed to speak to me, Monsieur d'Orléans, after what we have heard."

"What has been said that is so grave?"

"Where have you come from, if you please?"

"We've come from the council."

"But before the council?"

Orléans hesitated to reply. The smiling king poked the fire, and applauded himself silently for having for his wife a Lucretia, a presidente of the court of amour so severe for the conduct of a prince of the blood.

Fundamentally, Charles VI felt indulgent; he said to himself: *He's four years younger than me, with iron health, a fiery temperament and an imagination prompt to catch fire!* And the good brother, the good king, poked harder.

"But before the council?" repeated the queen, wounded by the prince's silence.

"Before the council, Madame, I witnessed the union of Mariette d'Anghuien with Messire Aubert Le Flamenc, one of my officers."

"It's true then? You don't deny it?"

"Why would I deny it? I'm astonished by your astonishment, Madame, since you have endowed the bride."

"I was pressed so insistently by you! But I did not know then why you were obstinate in making an unpleasant and ridiculous man marry that girl, and why she did not raise any obstacle to it."

"She has no fortune; I am giving her husband, Aubert Le Flamenc, a considerable fief, which will make her a lady of rank, and it's a fine match, in these times when there are few good ones."

"Ah! You're giving a fief to her husband? Who, then, claims that you have added to that the gift of an heir? That is worthy of a generous lord like you...of a..."

Isabeau was about to forget the presence of the king; her anger had carried her away. She stopped abruptly.

"You're joking, surely, Madame," said the Duc in an ambiguous one, calculated to warn the queen of her imprudence, while being wary of it.

Charles VI intervened, in a half-critical tone. "No, no, the queen isn't joking. Have you not, brother, as a suzerain, your *droit du seigneur?*"

"You might abolish it, Sire, if I did not make use of it. That would be poor recompense for a faithful servant."

"That's good, Louis, that's very good. I want the law to be respected under my reign, and you ought to set an example in that regard."

Isabeau, provoked by her husband as much as her lover, said, sharply: "What good are these semblances of morals, Monsieur d'Orléans? Can you not see that we know the whole story? And from whom did we obtain it? From another girl that you've abandoned."

"Who are you talking about?" D'Orléans seemed to be searching his memory in good faith.

"Who? You have so many? Coline Demerre! A double misdeed, a double crime, a double infamy!"

"By Phoebus, Madame, those are strong words for a very vulgar adventure."

"Yes," said the king, ceasing to poke the fire. "You're going too far, Isabelle." He stood up, pushed back his chair with his foot, and adopted a tone that was commanding as well as conciliatory. "I believe that you're joking, and you're both getting carried away. Louis, there's anger in your eyes, and there's anger in yours, Madame; it's almost a quarrel! Is there some novelty, then, in such an adventure in the French court? Thank God, for sins of amour, above all, there is remission. My edict against debauchery only concerns violence. If our first parents were punished for their disobedience, it was the woman who was punished primarily. We have added shame. It is up to her to watch over her honor constantly. Thus, where there is no employment of force, we have only criticism for a weapon. That being the case, according to the law, you are free, Madame, as presidente of the court of amour, to impose a fine upon Louis, but as sovereign, you ought to use in his favor the right of clemency, as I do myself, and let there be no further mention of it."

The queen yielded, frowning.

"Come on!" said Charles VI, playing his debonair role fully. "Shake hands cordially."

"There's no need," murmured Isabeau. "I shan't mention it again."

"The hand, damn it! Am I not the king? The hand! Ah, that's good. Lower your head, Madame, so that I can give you the kiss of peace. Now, I'll quit you in order to go and put order into our ball. It's the first of the carnival; I want it to be magnificent."

Satisfied with having rendered justice, Charles VI drew away, and for as long as his footsteps resounded on

43

the paving stones, the sullen pair remained mute, facing one another. As soon as the king could no longer be heard, the tone changed abruptly between Isabeau and Orléans; *tu* replaced *vous* and the quarrel was reignited.

"Are you mad, Isabeau," said the prince, "to speak before him as you did?"

"I could not retain my anger at a treason like yours. Now, if I listened any further, I'd lacerate your face with my fingernails."

"That's a very Germanic jealousy, my beauty. Our French ladies never lacerate anyone."

"That's because they love less."

"It's because they accommodate to life better. Let's speak frankly, my queen; in attaching myself to you, I haven't made a pact of servitude."

"Servitude is for me alone, then?"

"No more than for me. Full and entire liberty for both of us."

"Oh, you have no heart or soul!"

"I'll prove the contrary to you by reading you a ballad composed in your praise. Sit down there and listen."

"You're mocking! Louis, we are very guilty toward the king, and your conduct chastises me cruelly."

"Oh, not a word about that, my beautiful queen; amour and remorse don't rhyme. Listen to my verses instead."

"Louis, that girl you've married off—will she remain close to you?"

"That depends on her husband."

"Listen. Forgetfulness of your perfidy is on one condition. You've given them a fief; let them go to reside there tomorrow; I demand it."

"You're very suspicious, Isabelle. Won't the husband be there to guard his wife? He's one of my best officers."

"One of your most devoted, you mean? Devoted to the extent of shame."

"You're calumniating him."

"You're holding on, then, to that woman! I'll hold to what I said."

"So be it. Do as you like. But listen to my song."

"Songs indeed, your amour!"

"It's a difficult meter; furthermore, it's a crowned rhyme; it's an allegory, showing that it has been inspired by a queen!"

"Oh, I know you, frivolous rhymer! You don't like anything but noise, fêtes, everything that gleams and radiates, beautiful flowers, songs, gilded garments and new amours. Ferociously ambitious but without a goal, politicking solely to have the means of providing for your crazy expense, loving the arts out of idleness and vanity, a good knight in tourneys but fearing war for its fatigues, you've never had a passion for me that is worthy of me; you've loved me in passing, like any other little beauty, and here you are, already surprised and anxious about the imprudent awakened passion that responds to your caprice, whom you enlace, and whom you only perceive today as a bird extending its chain for the first time."

The queen was speaking the truth; the duc was anxious about that ardor; he wanted to defuse it.

"To speak for such a long time, it's at least necessary to sit down, Madame."

Pushing a seat toward the fireplace, Orléans let himself fall into it, started to poke the fire as his brother had done, and listened to the queen like a man resigned to an hour of ennui.

Isabeau did not perceive, or pretended not to perceive, that ennui. She continued her speech, as a woman determined to impose her will and to cause the duc, who disdained her for rivals unworthy of a queen, to lower his head.

"Will you never be sage Louis? If I thought that all that was just the lightness of youth, I'd be patient, for in my love for you there's a thought for the future. I'm not a seduced girl who's weeping, and whose honor can be saved by a marriage. For me to betray my duties as a wife and queen, it required a powerful charm, and woe betide you if, into the pact that binds us, you've only put a momentary whim! Personally, I've put all my soul into it, all my life in this world and my damnation in the other… perhaps."

At the final word, the duc raised his head, and lowered it again almost immediately, under the piercing gaze, which finished off ideas difficult to formulate in words.

Isabeau continued in a breathless voice: "Where has the desire to make you rich and powerful not drawn me? What have I not done to give you the authority in the kingdom that you enjoy, to the exclusion of the king's uncles and that Jean de Nevers, who is jealous of you and hates you? Shall I say it? In the deviation of my passion, entirely disinterested since it had no other end but your future, have I not sometimes dreamed that there is nothing between you and the throne but a feeble and sick king for whom death might perhaps be a benefit, if it were gentle and slow…?"

Orléans sat up straight and, recoiling in fear, clamored rather than said: "What are you saying, Madame?"

"I love you to that extent," said Isabeau, coldly.

"What is such a love, then? It frightens me. Have we reverted to the kings of the first dynasty? Do you want to fuse the name of Isabeau de Bavière with those of Brunehaut and Frédégonde?"

"Ah! You think you can play with impunity with the happiness of a woman like me, wrench her away from virtue and then reject her like a flower whose perfume you've respired? No, no. Once launched by you outside the path of good, I've felt new faculties awakening in my soul. Ambition has seized me, in seeing power escaping from the hands of my husband to return to his uncles: an ambition that will be all to your advantage, if you wish, or of which you will only be the instrument. Choose! But know that retreat is impossible."

"Madame, you're frightening me and desolating me. What burden do you want to impose on my idleness, my insouciance? If I've raised my voice in the council, if I've even taken some part in public affairs, it has only ever been to sustain the privileges of the nobility, so frequently attacked in recent times, and to prevent war, which I hate with all my heart. But to aspire to power! To try the crown on my head! Why, Madame it wouldn't hold there; it would fall around my neck like the collar of a slave."

The queen covered her face with her hands and murmured: "Crown or collar, you'll try it."

At that moment, the duc's favorite page, who had scratched at the door, entered the room and went straight to his master.

"What do you want with me, page?"

The page slid a letter swiftly into the prince's hand, whispering: "On the part of the Duchesse de Nevers, Monseigneur." Then, in a loud voice, seeming only to be delivering the latter message: "Messire Aubert Le Flamenc and his wife are asking to be presented to you."

"Tell them to wait! I'm with Madame la Reine!"

"Let them come in," said Isabeau.

"Oh well, let them in!" sad Louis, insouciantly.

When the page had left, Isabeau de Bavière hastened to add, in an imperative voice: "Let them come in, and let them depart immediately afterwards for their fief, do you hear!"

Then, without waiting for the duc's response, she drew away precipitately.

IV. MARIETTE D'ANGHUIEN

Oh, let me flee you; there is still time.
Later, I could not; later, despite my vows,
Dying, I would say: I love you, I adore you!
And if I succumbed, would you be happier?

As he read the missive brought by his page, Louis d'Orléans, with his habitual lightness, gave no further thought to the tantrum of the daughter of Étienne II, comte palatine of the Rhine, and Tasée Visconti. He needed not to think about the ascendant step that, via adultery, was pushing Isabeau to regicide…from which she would subsequently be preserved by the madness of the king.

In fact, Charles VI, in dementia, left the government in the hands of his wife.

Louis d'Orléans, who was to be the father of a poet of great renown, Charles d'Orléans, was also a poet in his time, but he was above all a man frantic for pleasures, with intermittences of piety. Amorous by temperament, with prejudice of race, he became infatuated with brunettes and blondes, noblewomen or bourgeoises, daughters of the city or vassals of the fields; all of them possessed the same right to his temporary affection.

A well-furnished bosom, a shapely waist or a well-made leg attracted him and delighted him. A pretty hand or a dainty foot enchanted him. Orléans dreamed of all that while reading Marguerite de Hainaut's epistle, because Marguerite united all of it.

But the appearance of Mariette d'Anghuien, followed by her husband, made him forget the charming dream for the proximal reality.

"Approach, Aubert, and you, *our* genteel wife..."

The plural *our* did not strike the husband at all, but caused the wife to blush, only making her seem prettier in consequence.

"Well," the duc continued, "has my chaplain. Père Legrand, sermonized you well? I quit the place once the mass was said, for if he had perceived me at his homily, that rival of Canon Gerson[20] would have subjected me to a long remonstration, for the luxury of my garments."

"I suppose, Monseigneur, that he would only have done so in order to put in regard your nobility of soul and your generosity," replied Aubert.

"Aubert, I have made you the investiture of the fief of Cauny, near Nogent-sur-Marne, in the dependency of my Château de Beauté. I wanted, while giving you the title and revenue of that fief, to keep you close to me, but an unexpected occurrence has changed my opinion. You will go to live in your manor tomorrow."

"What, Monseigneur! Oh, that pains me!"

"It's decided. But I often go to my Château de Beauté, when hunting in the Bois de Vincennes, which is very close to your fief, and I shall summon you to my side. Go therefore, Sire de Cauny, to make your adieux

---

[20] Jean Gerson (1363-1429) was appointed as Chancellor of the University of Paris in 1395, when he became a powerful and influential voice for social reform. He supported Christine de Pizan in attaching the casual morality of *Roman de la rose*, and similarly became famous as a defender of Jeanne d'Arc, endorsing her supernatural vocation.

to your relatives and friends, and put your other affairs in order, if you have any. Go."

"Thank you, Monseigneur; I shall use the permission. If you'll permit it, my wife can stay in the waiting room until I return."

"Leave your wife here. This room is well heated. She'll be much more comfortable...I have a few words to say to her on behalf of the queen, who has endowed her."

Aubert bowed, and went out in a very dignified manner. The title of Sire de Cauny had made him another man—which is to say that the borrowed dignity, grafted on to his military bearing and his grotesque physiognomy, rendered him even more ridiculous than he really was. A soldier with a beard and moustache, at first sight he was repulsive; his bronzed hands caused little muscles to protrude like the roots of an oak tree, and announced a Herculean strength. His vulgar physiognomy, burned by the sun, was no less rugged than the bark of a centenarian cedar. His red hair, badly combed, like a clump of brushwood, framed cheeks veined with feverish redness, like autumn leaves. His large feet seemed to bite the ground. When he marched he produced the sound of a pick-ax. When he was standing motionless under arms, one might have thought that he had taken root in the earth. His gaze, as brilliant as the reflection of an incendiary torch, denoted both a naïve, limitless confidence, and the fulgurance of a ferocious character, depending on circumstances.

Certainly the Prince of Fools was not an Adonis, and he was endowed with an uncommon physical strength, but he was far from having the ugliness and musculature of Captain Aubert. There was another difference, even more marked, between the two men, externally maltreated by nature. That was a great intelligence in the clown and an implacable obstinacy in the soldier. The former laughed at his enemy, and showered him with barbed epigrams; the later meditated for a long time the blow he wanted to strike; his crossbow took aim, whistled, hit the target, and the enemy fell, not to rise again...as you shall see in due course.

As soon as he no longer heard the pick-ax blows of the Sire du Cauny, who drew away striking the paving stones, Louis d'Orléans set about contemplating Mariette d'Anghuien with a gaze of new lust and new surprise, as if he were seeing her for the first time.

Would one believe it? He had a momentary scruple; then, after a moment, he said to himself: *Bah! Amour is amour, and amity is only a shadow. Alain Chartier can claim as much as you like that "the devotion of a veritable friend is as noble as martyrdom"; it's doubtless a beautiful thought, but my devoted Le Flamenc's wife is even more beautiful.*

Thus argued the king's brother, who, not having been stopped by that axiom when it was a matter of seducing his sister-in-law, was certainly not going to put the friendship of the Sire de Cauny in parallel with the amity of a brother.

His ardent gaze covered the young woman in her bridal costume, a simple dress, in good taste for the epoch, bringing out the mat white of her shoulders and the ash blonde of her silken hair, undulating around a gracious face imprinted with languor and melancholy.

Pensive and plaintive, Mariette remembered her primitive purity. The retained emotion of her nuptial benediction lent her gaze a veiled and timid expression that made her a new creature in the eyes of her seducer. It seemed to the poor seduced woman that a new baptism had purified her and that, retracing her steps, she had reentered the chaste life of her early years. However, she shuddered and desired the reality of something unknown, which she glimpsed vaguely through maternal sensations: a gilded dream, the scintillation of a star whose gleam pierced the light and silky fabric of the veil ornamenting her marital crown.

"Mariette," said he prince, drawing nearer, "you're remaining silent and seem very sad. However, I've acted in accordance with your desires and you know whether I've done my best. Does your husband displease you? He's a simple man whom you can guide as you wish. I chose a man of that nature in order that you'd be less hindered. He was a captain in my arbalestiers. I took him out a little while ago in order to attach him to my person; his face amused me."

"Ah! Perhaps, indeed..."

"As for what embarrasses you, you'll pretext a vow to the Virgin; that will suffice. Were you counting on remaining next to me? I'm suffering more than you, but it can't be."

"Monseigneur, I prefer that it is as you have decided. I will admit that Père Legrand's discourse has moved me, and I've resolved no longer to deceive the man who has thrown a veil over my shame."

"Oh, my darling, my beauty, that's not our convention! Great God, do you think I'll abandon you thus? It's only to your supplications and the dread that you have of your family that I've yielded in permitting this marriage, but don't believe that you have become indifferent to me. I only love you; for you I would sacrifice the love of a queen..."

As he spoke, the duc turned his gaze toward the entrance door, as if he feared that Isabeau de Bavière had remained on the threshold. He saw nothing, but a gust of music arrived to surprise him.

"Ah!" said the duc, after a moment's reflection, "I remember; there's a ball in the house this evening; you'll be there; it will distract you, and tomorrow I'll take you to your manor personally, without any ceremony, as if I were going hunting. No one will see anything in that,"

"No, no, Monseigneur," said Mariette, "my resolution is made. It's enough that I'm hiding from Messire Aubert a secret that doesn't belong entirely to me. I fear, by revealing it, transforming your grateful servant into a mortal enemy. I'm entirely his henceforth. He might have found a purer wife, but none more faithful."

Mariette trembled in her energy.

"You're afflicting me Mariette. If that's the effect of the sermon, it won't last, unless you're gripped by a beautiful passion for your Vulcan. Caprices of that sort have been seen... in mythology... but Christians don't prefer ugliness to what is good."

"How can you joke like that, Monseigneur?"

"What do you want me to joke about, if not a grotesque husband? But the music's growing louder; one might imagine that it's coming this way. In fact, the gallery is lighting up...the crowd will soon invade the Hôtel Saint-Pol, I don't know why my brother doesn't take his court to the Palais des Tournelles. Here, one is truly cramped when there's merriment and feasting. Come, my beauty; take my arm. Let's get away from a room where our conversation would soon have witnesses."

"Where are you taking me? To my husband?"

"Yes, yes, come on. A curse on importunates! A curse on the stupid people who are driving us to this!"

Chatting in low voices, Orléans and Mariette traversed rooms variously ornamented by the Prince of Fools

and stopped in one of them that was of colossal propor-
tions. Frescoes due to the brush of Jehan Muret, and arabesques snaked in the friezes with mingled garlands of
amours with inflated cheeks fluttering in pinions under
rich drapes of crimson damask, fabric brought back from
the Orient by princes returning from the crusades. The
lower borders were framed by a large strip of tropical
hardwood, on which two rows of Gothic ornaments were
sculpted. All around, the walls, covered with gilded
Flanders leather, skillfully decorated sideboards, creden-
zas and delicately-wrought dressers could be seen. On
the shelves of the dressers, golden and silver vessels glit-
tered amid crystal and porcelain.

Among those riches there was an object precious by
virtue of its rarity. It was a Venetian glass in an ebony
frame thirty-three centimeters high and broad, a glass
that served Isabeau de Bavière as a mirror. Later, it
would render the same service to Marguerite d'Anjou,
the wife of Charles VII. The chronicle does not say
whether Agnès Sorel reflected her image in it, but it as-
serts that Louis XI consulted it often, in order to make
certain that Olivier le Daim, his barber, had shaved him
perfectly. From king to king that object reached François
I. Under that gallant king, whose court had almost become an Oriental harem, the mirror served many times
to frame the pretty faces of noblewomen and the little
band that followed the court of that "slightly lewd"
monarch, as Juvénal des Ursins put it,[21] and finally
Catherine de Medicis, who possessed it, took pleasure

---

[21] Jean Juvénal des Ursins (1388-1473), who eventually rose
through the ranks of the Church to be Archbishop of Reims
was the reputed author of *Histoire de Charles VI Roy de
France*, one of the principal sources for the present novel.

not only in seeing it reproduce her features, her beautiful breasts and her beautiful hands but also her beautiful legs, of which she was very proud, Brantôme says.[22] She showed them at every opportunity, going up and down staircases, traversing a stream, dancing, and even sitting down nonchalantly in a Gothic seat, a sort of bed of repose serving as a sofa. Brantôme does not tell us whether Catherine saw reflected in that mirror—preserved to our days, since it can be seen in the Louvre museum— the dagger that pierced Coligny and gave the signal for the massacre of the Huguenots.

At any rate, at the moment when Orléans and Mariette made the inspection of such beautiful and rare things, relative to the century in which they lived, at the very moment when Louis de France was admiring the pretty face of Madame de Cauny in the limpid water of the little glass, when he was taking advantage the non-arrival, as yet, of the guests of the fête to give Mariette a kiss that made her crimson and rendered her even more beautiful, Aubert Le Flamenc, having concluded his affairs, was returning to the Hôtel Saint-Pol, traversing narrow, muddy and poorly lit streets.

A few provostal orders had appeared, on the subject of the Parisian aedility, but no one took any account of them. The question had been mooted of paving the streets, in which pigs were allowed to circulate, wallowing in the mud, but that order from the provost of Paris was still in the planning stage. Another edict intimated an order to every bourgeois to sweep outside his door, which did not prevent the streets from remaining very dirty, and as the inspection of doorsteps and public

---

[22] Pierre de Bourdeille, seigneur de Brantôme (c.1540-1614) was an exceedingly unreliable historian.

squares was not anyone's responsibility, Paris became a receptacle of filth.

As for street-lighting, the usage was introduced much later. A regulation obliged all the inhabitants to place candles in their windows at six o'clock in the evening in winter and after nine o'clock in summer, but in the winter the cold was assumed to have extinguished the candles and in summer, people relied on the moon, to the point that the Prince of Fools, who was on the look-out for anything that might be lucrative without much trouble, and useful to his theater, asked for and obtained from Queen Isabeau de Bavière the privilege of hiring out lanterns of which he was the inventor; they were made of tin-plate cut out and fitted with panes of polished horn, garnished with candle-stubs. To that effect he established shops in every corner of Paris where men and children were stationed, ready to accompany persons passing by on foot, on horseback or in carriage, with the lanterns, in exchange for a fee.

Aubert Le Flamenc was, therefore, going to retrieve his wife from the Hôtel de Saint-Pol, tottering, with a profound scorn for the straight line, for copious libations with relatives, friends and acquaintances had multiplied to such a extent that the old soldier, in spite of his aptitude to support the impact of full glasses, had clinked too many. In spite of that, without the bad state of the streets, without the heaps of rubbish, and without the pools of stagnant water, in which he sank up to his knees, without the stray dogs, cats, mice and pigs lying in the gutter, but above all without the four burly fellows who were following in his tracks and who, at the corner of a street blacker than the others threw over him what was the known as the "sheet of the dead," he would probably have reached the palace of Charles VI safe and sound. He would not have served as the butt of the mirth of the courtiers and, on the other hand, France might not have fallen prey to the English, so much can the smallest cases have great effects, and so true is it that the destiny that hangs over States takes pleasure in putting the fate of peoples in the hands of a monster or a madman.

Hazard gave the Roman Empire to Nero; and Charles VI, King of France by heredity, a sage, economical, pious, political, just and prudent prince, firm in council, intrepid for good, might have been spared shameful and dolorous pages in history without the crazy scheme of the Prince of Fools, which put the realm within an inch of its doom and condemned that king to forty-six years of physical and mental suffering.

V. NEVERS AND ORLÉANS

...I do not want renown
I do not want, myself, to rise to the skies.
I only want to love, and above all to be loved.
To remain a wife down here, What more can one desire?

"I know something sweeter than the summer breeze, gentler than a bee kissing the calyx of a flower, more charming than a moss rose in an islet of verdure; I know something more enviable than the sinuosities of leafy valleys: it is a dazzling ball, a spray of human flowers, brunette and blonde women, rosy and white..."

So said Alain Chartier in the middle of the crowd at the ball, giving his arm to Christine de Pisan, the beautiful Venetian who had come to France as a child with her father, the astrologer of Charles V, a poet wife, now the widow, of a Picard gentleman, to whom Charles V gave from his treasury a pension of two hundred livres.

While waiting for the Prince of Fools' musicians to give the signal for the dance, the crowd followed the two poets, who had been recognized beneath the masks

Master Gonin had other preoccupations for the moment. His obsession was lucre, and he had no more scruples than the legendary Till Uspiegel, alias Uspiegle, to whom Germany, Flanders and Poland disputed the honor of having give birth, and who amused himself robbing passers-by in the Black Forest.[23] He, the king's fool, robbed the court from time to time.

---

[23] The picaresque and scatologically-obsessed tale of Till Eulenspiegel—usually translated literally into English as

Perfectly disguised and made up, he was conversing in a corner with a relative by the name of Étienne Mustau.

"You see, cousin," he said, "at the court it's not only necessary to seize the shepherd's hour. Tonight I shall slip all the way to Madame la Reine, who won't fail to compliment me on the organization of the fête. I shall take advantage of that to introduce you, and as I know that she's ready to give preference to the first comer, in order to replace the king of the ribauds, whom she despises because of a certain adventure in which he has been indiscreet, you're sure of your affair.

"I understand," replied Mustau, a low Norman for whom the queen's écus and gold florins were not to be disdained, "but is the responsibility difficult to fulfill?"

"Not at all! Otherwise, I wouldn't propose it to you."

"Thank you," replied the Norman, lifting up his hat with turned-up wings, with a clawed hand, in order to salute him in a mocking fashion.

"And as, furthermore," Gonin continued, "you can render us important services…"

"Yes, indeed, but I'd like to know exactly what the fruits and duties of that royalty are."

"The duties are forming the police of the Hôtel Saint-Pol and assisting in all the arrests made by the provost of Paris. The fruits are thirteen deniers a year and forty Parisian sols for your robe and your valet."

"That's not much."

"Owlglass," although that probably overlooks a fecal *double entendre*—originates from a chapbook published in the early sixteenth century, but the events it relates are set in the fourteenth.

"Plus a contribution of five sols from all the women with gilded belts…"

"That's better," said the Norman, smiling, "The game's abundant."

"Plus the clothes of all those you take to be hanged."

"Oho!"

"Plus, finally, an even better advantage, about which we'll talk at a more useful time."

With that, the Prince of Fools returned to the platform where his orchestra was perched, and, in the time it took for him to give a few orders to his musicians while waiting the order himself from Sir Hugues de Guisay to have them put their instruments to work, the crowd grew, while Orléans and Mariette strolled through the masked or unmasked waves, still conversing on the same theme.

"You see, dear Madame de Cauny," said the prince, "I'll take your bulldog to one side and inform him of the role that he has to play. Gold! As much as he wants! What man of that species doesn't dance in the fashion one wishes to the music of golden sheep?"

"I can't hear that kind of talk about the man whose name I bear."

"Bah! He's only noble by virtue of the fief I've given him, for he isn't by birth. He's no more than a peasant; his family has been in the possession of judiciary charges for a long time. We call that a man of mixed race. By the way, what's become of him? It isn't appropriate that we stroll for a long time without him, His absence will embarrass us."

"He must be waiting, Monseigneur, in the hall where he left us. I'll go see if he's there."

"Go, my darling, and come back quickly."

So saying, the duc accompanied Mariette as far as one of the doors, where he quit her, not without having collected, in passing, the words of his uncles and his aunts, who were chatting with Charles de Savoisy, making the observation that the kingdom would soon be populated entirely by Orléans' bastards.

The Duc de Nevers came in with the Sire de Guisay.

"You here, my cousin!" said the prince, going straight to his enemy. "What a surprise! Agreeable as it is, it would be even more so of you had brought our amiable relative, your beloved wife."

"Yes, it's me; I changed my mind," retorted to duc. "Before quitting France for Hungary I wanted to be in a situation to compare the elegance of the court of Charles VI with that of Sigismund's court."

"It's for that reason that it would have been appropriate to bring our cousin. Women are better judges of that than we are."

Without replying, Bourgogne took Sire Hugues' arm again. They drew away.

"Bull!" murmured Orléans. "Go combat the infidels; you won't kill them all."

He was laughing as he strolled when a masked woman in a black domino came to lean her arm on his, whispering her name in his ear.

"You here, Marguerite!" he said, in a stifled voice.

"Didn't I inform you by my note?"

"Of course, but your husband is in the house."

"He can't suspect me in this disguise."

"He'd kill you, the brute!"

"Well, I'd be dying for you."

"But I don't want you to die."

"I've come to tell you that if he forces me to accompany him to Hungary, you won't lose me entirely. Here, keep this."

And Madame de Nevers slipped into Orléans' hand a minuscule portrait painted by Jehan Muret, who had, as I mentioned, taught the duc to paint on porcelain.

"It's a good resemblance, my adored Marguerite."

"Adieu, Louis. Prudence demands that I withdraw."

"Alas! Losing you so soon! I'll escort you back to the Hotel d'Artois."

"What folly!"

"Come."

Orléans tried in vain to open a passage through the crowd, which formed a wall, everyone trampling feet in order to hold his place and lose nothing of the promised masquerade. Had not the Prince of Fools not sworn to surpass himself? While waiting for an exit to appear, the duc searched for means of obtaining another rendezvous.

"Marguerite," he said, after a minute's reflection, "take this little golden key, the masterpiece of an artisan of Bruges. It opens without effort the postern of my Château de Beauté that gives access to the vicinity of the Chapelle de Saint-Saturnin, where your husband can't prevent you from going to pray for the success of the Hungarian expedition..."

The duchesse only just had time to seize and secrete the little key that Orléans held out to her before a woman, heavily ornamented, not disguised but masked, who had cleared a path to reach them by means of a prodigy of will, loomed up before them like a threat and retained the duchesse by her monkish robe—for the domino was no more than that—and said in a tremulous voice: "Duc! You have the appearance of a marauding wolf arrested in its flight. Who is this ewe whose fleece is so soft?"

Silk was not known then; it was scarcely found until the reign of Charles VIII; the word "fleece" was therefore exact.

At the first word, Orléans had recognized Isabeau de Bavière.

The latter crumpled and tugged the woolen robe, as if to tear it.

"Can it be Mariette d'Anghuien?" the queen continued. "Or Coline Demerre, or Madame de Maulevrier? Oh, the rosary is long in the telling!"

"Madame," replied Louis, "would you think it good that someone penetrated the enigma under which that strange blonde hair is sheltering, those blue eyes that launch lightning flashes, that swan's neck and that waist in which flexibility is allied with majesty?"

"I'll break my incognito; let the same be done for me."

She let go of the robe in order to take off her mask. The duchesse recoiled. Orléans would not have succeeded in distancing her far enough if the queen, in trying to untie the string of her mask had not tightened the knot. While she was trying to break the knot, momentarily blinded, Orléans had a flash of audacious genius. He saw Jean de Bourgogne a few paces away and took his wife to him swiftly.

"My cousin," he said, nobly, "I'm addressing myself to your chivalry. I have powerful reasons for this lady to remain unknown. Promise that you will have her mask respected. My litter is at the door of the house; take Madame to it without addressing a word to her. Will you do that?"

"You're mistaking me for the Prince of Fools," growled Bourgogne.

"I'm taking you for a general to whom I'll have more troops given than he asked of me."

"That's good," said Nevers.

Presenting his bony and hairy hand to the lady trembling in her woolen robe, without the slightest suspicion that the little hand enclosed in his, like a fine diamond in a case, was that of his wife, he opened a gap in the crowd with a gesture.

The movement had been so prompt and the surprise, above all, so great for Isabeau that the latter, unmasked, suffocated with fury for two minutes before advancing to say to the prince, almost aloud: "Perfidy! Treason!"

"Isabeau! Contain yourself. It's the last time I shall find myself with her."

"Mariette! It was her, then?"

"Yes."

"Ah! You've brought her here! Is it true that you won't see her again?"

"It's true."

"Why isn't she with her husband?"

"She's going to join him."

"And it's Nevers who is doing the honors of her conduct?"

"Undoubtedly."

"Ah! You're lying!" said Isabeau, who saw at that very moment Mariette entering the ballroom, having searched for the Sire de Cauny in vain. "You always lie! But I shall know who the other is!"

She launched herself toward the exit. Orléans tried to retain her, but the precaution was superfluous, for Nevers came back in and Isabeau, forcing the prince to give her free passage, went past Duc Jean without perceiving him.

Bourgogne said to Orléans, simply: "It's done. That's worth a good twelve hundred lances."

"I give you my word, you'll have them."

"Thank you."

VI. THE MASQUERADE

Like a red serpent formless and immeasurable,
Now fire suddenly emerges, hissing.

In a matter of minutes Orléans had felt all the anguish and nightmares of a frightful dream. Isabeau un-
masking the duchesse before the duc was the culmina-
tion of horror for him, for the court, for the royalty.

He pulled himself together rapidly when Bourgogne
had thanked him.

The Prince of Fools' orchestra, interrupting its
dancing harmony with a discordant sound of instruments
mingled with voices crying "Charivari!" announced the
entrance of the impatiently-awaited masquerade.

It was composed of six masked satyrs, followed by
several similarly masked individuals in grotesque costumes, holding kitchen utensils and carrying flamboyant
resinous torches.

At the center of that masquerade, on a species of
palanquin, Aubert Le Flamenc advanced, cursing and
swearing, escorted and held prisoner by the four body-
guards who had abducted him. He was decked in a long
black robe strewn with horns embroidered in white
wool, his head coiffed in an ox-head bonnet. Behind him
came two other individuals, one wearing a miter ornamented with the antlers of a stag, the other carrying a
rosier terminated by two ram's horns.

Trumpets sounded fanfares every time the Sire de
Cauny gave evidence of wanting to utter words of revolt.
Around the masquerade, six companies of the queen's
maids of honor and the king's pages, clad in German,

67

Italian and Spanish fashion, commenced their gallant choreographic evolutions, to the sound of tambourines, simulating a combat of risqué steps, finishing with the incisive acclamation: "Charivari!" which the spectators repeated in echoes.

Then came the leaps, the feats of strength and skill, by the children of the Prince of Fools, costumed as mythological gods, light-footed fauns, satyrs with horned heads, rivers crowned with marine rushes, woodland goddesses, dryads, hamadryads, naiads, oreads and napées, quivering to the sound of buccinas. All those gods and goddesses wore gaudy garments woven in gold and silver fabrics, fake but very shiny; others were hidden under the cardboard and cloth of fantastic monsters, wild beasts of the woods, deformed habitants of the earth, the air and the waters: vultures, eagles griffons, including a braying donkey and a pig wagging its tail while squealing, all the way to a cock launching its strident cry into the vast hall, mingled with the mewling of a concert of cats, perfectly imitated.

No charivari had ever been more perfect than that one, promulgated by the court of amour of the court of France, without being registered, and which is reproduced historically.

Thus far, Orléans, who had approached Mariette, had not suspected that he had an interest in that masquerade. The noise was deafening, but if it prevented him from conversing it did not prevent him from miming with his gaze and the pressure of his fingers what he could not say. But by the silence that suddenly fell, even on the part of Aubert Le Flamenc, gagged expressly, the attention of the prince was awakened, and it was no longer permissible for him to be distracted.

The chamberlain Savoisy, playing the part of one of the satyrs, spoke in a loud voice, but with a disguised voice: "This is to announce the consecration of Messire Aubert Le Flamenc to the dignity of Bishop of the Horned, which he has merited by his marriage with Damoiselle Mariette d'Anghuien."

"By God's blood! Wretches!" Orléans vociferated. But he interrupted himself, because Mariette fainted and he had to sustain her.

The crowd cried: "Charivari!" and the queen, having returned from her hunt, called to him violently, saying; "Prince, listen, like us! Await your part."

Savoisy went on: "By the sentence of the court of amour, the candidate here present will receive the consecration from the hands of Monseigneur le Duc d'Orléans, who will present him with the insignia, the miter of stag's antlers and the crosier of ram's horns."

Sniggers burst forth.

Exasperated, Orléans launched himself toward the satyrs, tore away the torch that a valet was carrying and brandished it.

"This is an infamous farce!" he cried. "Who are the insensates who are attacking my honor thus and that of Madame de Cauny? I swear to God that no one will leave here without learning what is owed to a son of France. Come on, masks off!"

A burst of laughter having replied to that exclamation, as he was preparing to join action to words, the prince encountered before him, instead of the six satyrs, who had slipped away, six new individuals dressed in coats of cloth to which were fixed, with wax, threads of cotton "in the form and color of tresses," according to

Froissart's expression.[24] Tresses is only a euphemism here; it is necessary to read it as coarse hair.

This improvised savages, hairy from the top of the head to the soles of the feet, were none other than Charles VI himself; the Comte de Join, "a young and genteel knight;" Messire Charles de Poitiers, the son of the Comte de Valentinois; Messire Yvain de Galles, the bastard of Foix; a young knight, the son of the Seigneur de Nantouillet; and Hugues de Guisay.

D'Orléans ran at one of them, and the fire "entered into the cotton," Froissart recounts:

The flame heated the wax by which the cotton was attached to the cloth; the cotton and waxed chemises were dried and loosened, and joined to the flesh, and caught fire ardently. And those who were dressed in them, who felt the anguish, began crying out bitterly and horribly, and there was so much mischief that no one dared approach them...

The Duchesse de Berry delivered the king from that peril, for she bundled him under her cotillon and covered him in order to put out the fire, and said to him, for the king wanted to pull away from her by force: "Where are you trying to go? You can see your companions burning? Who are you? It's time you named yourself."

"I'm the king."

---

[24] The famous *Chronicles* of Jean Froissart (1337-1405) are one of the principal sources of the present novel. They relate that Orléans did pick up a torch as he entered the fête belatedly and accidentally started a fire in which the casualties named herein were burned, but the addition of Aubert Le Flamenc to the scene is, of course, entirely fictitious.

"Ha! Go away, Monsieur, to put on other clothes, and make sure that the queen sees you, for she is very anxious for you."

Is it necessary to embroider upon Froissart's sketch in order to depict the tumult and the din of that scene, in which nearly eight hundred people were precipitated in torrents through three or four issues, pressing, climbing over one another, howling, blaspheming, shoving, trampling one another underfoot, as in every melee in which egotism cries: "Every man for himself!" and in which one only hears one single cry among a thousand?

"Fire!"

"Fire!"

"Save the king!"

"I'm burning!"

"Water!"

"The king was in the masquerade!"

"Monseigneur d'Orléans has set fire to his brother's clothes!"

"Regicide!"

"Fratricide!"

Those cries emerged from the Hôtel Saint-Pol and flew toward Paris.

Aubert Le Flamenc, whose Herculean strength had been suppressed until then by the equal force if the four mercenaries, who ran away at the first cries of alarm, rid himself of his bonds, removed his gag and, running to the unconscious Mariette, picked her up, crossed the distance that separated him from the main entrance to the Hôtel de Saint-Pol in a few bounds and emerged, charged with his precious burden.

In the meantime, the pyramidal dresser whose nine shelves were buckling under the weight of the king's tableware—dishes, plates, sold gold ewers, cups and jugs of various forms—was not sheltered from serious attaints.

"Hey, cousin," said Étienne Mustau to the Prince of Fools, "your musicians are pillaging the dresser.

"They'll make great lords, those poor serfs," replied Gonin, in a compassionate tone. He added: "You have a vulgar fashion of talking, cousin. Those fellows are hermetic philosophers practicing alchemy."

"Ah yes, the Great Work!"

"Precisely. They're skipping alembics. You'll see many others."

"When I'm charged with the policing of the palace, you mean?"

"You comprehend marvelously."

"One is either Norman or one isn't."

"Oh, you certainly are. Poor king! Poor realm of France! Every man for himself."

"Except you, cousin."

Meanwhile, the rumors continued. There was talk of five or six dead, including Sire Hugues de Guisay. As for the king, he had been transported in all haste to his apartments, and demands were being made in vain for his astrological physician, who was no longer in the house.

"Since we have nothing to do here, not having the right to dispose of the living to make dead men of then, and our astrology forbids us to be physicians, let's get out," said the Prince of Fools.

As they left the Hôtel Saint-Pol they crossed the path of Master Jehan Coquerel, Jean de Nevers' physician, summoned in all haste to replace the absent royal physician.

VII. THE KING'S DEMENTIA

The moon gives to those she loves
Glory, the purple and a diadem,
To make a conqueror of a churl
And transmute lead into gold.

Not far from the Hôtel Saint-Pol, built in order to be, according to the terms of the edict of 1364, "the solemn house of great frolics," facing the Palais des Tournelles and near the Bastille, simultaneously a prison and a fortress, stood a solid wall extending from the Rue Saint-Denis to the Arsenal. It was the defense of the palace even more than the defense of Paris.

At each of the corners of the house there was a tower into which one penetrated by a low door of solid iron. The principal tower, larger than the other three, with walls three meters thick, contained two bedrooms reserved for the royal couple. Although the first was poorly ornamented and dusty, scarcely furnished with a bed of obsolete form veiled with old curtains, the second was sumptuous, with its sculpted ebony furniture and its curtains representing Biblical scenes. Facing a silver Christ, admirably worked, which dominated a prie-dieu, also in ebony, was a fine portrait of Étienne II, Isabeau's father, painted by a Flemish artist

On the king's large bed, with twisted columns and a back with Gothic ailerons, taking up half the room—an apartment within an apartment, so to speak—Charles VI had been laid down, giving no sign of life. Chamberlain Savoisy and the secretary Alain Chartier had carried him through the debris of the conflagration all the way to this chamber, where all the courtiers who had not been in-jured had followed them, lamenting in the midst of the lamentations of the Duc d'Orléans, the innocent cause of the catastrophe.

In the midst of that consternation, a valet came to announce to Isabeau de Bavière, who was prostrate at her husband's beside, that for want of the king's physi-cian, Monsieur le Duc de Nevers' physician was asking to be admitted.

"Come in, Jehan!" cried Bourgogne. "And with the aid of God, save the king our sire!"

Immediately, everyone stood aside to leave the field free for Master Coquerel.

Ignorance and conceit were the master qualities of that empiric, expectorating at every opportunity the Lat-in of his vintage. So much for his mentality; physically, he was long in the torso and lower legs, short in the things and stout in the belly, with a oval face terminated in a goat's beard, a low brow, shining eyes and a shrill voice. For the sake of prestige he dressed in a necro-mancer's robe and ran around like a Basque afflicted by what is known in Navarre as *tirrinteria*, the habitual ma-laise of the colicky, according to Froissart.

"Have no fear, Monseigneur," replied Coquerel, "*Ressuscitabo Regem!* First—here's serpent powder: *pulvis reptilus!*"

He took from his satchel a little kettle, from which he took a pinch of powder, and presented the remedy to the Duchesse de Bourbon, who held out her hands to him.

"*Aqua et ignis!*" he clamored thereafter. "Bring the ewer and stoke up the fire."

He took the ewer from the hands of the Duchesse de Berry, as hasty as the Duchesse de Bourbon, and having filled the kettle with water, he had the Duchesse d'Anjou put it on the fire, while the three ducs, their husbands, reanimated the fire in the hearth, blowing in turn through an iron tube.

Coquerel was radiant with pride in having the highest persons in the land for servants,

While he took out a lancet in order to bleed the king, a new individual irrupted into the room. It was Master Guillaume Harsely, physician to the Duc d'Orléans. He knew other things that Coquerel, but was similarly ignorant. Their physique was as discordant as their knowledge Harsely was then shriveled to the bone, his head as hairy as Absalom's, his face like a razor blade, with a prominent nose on which a pair of large spectacles vacillated. He launched himself forward, as if to cleave an odious rival with his impact.

"What do I see? What is this? Master Coquerel here, with his lancet and jar of ointment? May the great Averroes aid me!"

"Master Guillaume," replied Conquerel, "I arrived before you, and you will not disavow the means I employ. Every malady, according to Hippocrates, comes from the derangement of the equilibrium of the fluids. Here the red face announces inflammation and engorgement of the blood. In that case, it is necessary to evacuate that liquid by a bleeding, *usque ad deliquium*, according to Galen, and to make use of refreshing medicaments."

"Galen lied through his teeth!"

"Galen lied?"

"You Galen is vagabond, a jacques, a maillotin!"

"Blasphemer!"

"And Hippocrates too…"

The two doctors were about to grab one another by the hair when it was pointed out to them that the king had great need of their aid. They hesitated to grab one another, but they continued the dispute.

Coquerel vociferated: "To call Hippocrates and Galen jacques and maillotins, who are the king's enemies!"

"I mean," said Harsely, trying to inflate himself, "that their medicine is only good for the people, only consisting of common drugs and bleeding, which barbers do in the marketplace and steam-bath attendants in their steam-baths. Such a treatment does not befit a person of noble blood, much less royal blood! Such maladies require precious remedies, like wine mixed with silver powder, *vinum argentatum*, or a dissolution of strong gold chains, and better still of true diamonds, as Chauliac[25] recommends, in palm wine, or some application of constellated stones, *gemmae constellatae*, in uneven number."

The verbiage flattered vanity, and the vain did not sense its stupidity. A murmur of approval welcomed it. Only Bourgogne remained impassive.

A new individual arrived, tall and fat, with a pale, full face, a thick beard and a solemn gait. It was the Milanese Rugiero, astrologer and physician to Charles VI.

"*Optime!*" he cried. "Yes, Master Harsely, your thesis is excellent, but on condition of not omitting the con-

---

[25] The physician Guy de Chauliac (c.1300-1368), author of *Chirurgia Magna*, which became a standard reference book in the fifteenth century, although modern historians doubt that he ever practiced surgery. He did, however, observe and document the Black Death and made the distinction between Bubonic Plague and Pneumonic Plague that persisted for centuries.

junction of the stars. To the devil with the Galenic donkey, who is only god to treat animals."

"A donkey, me!" riposte the Duc de Bourgogne's physician. "A donkey, me, who possesses geomancy, hydromancy and pyromancy! Let God save the king, if he can, without me! *Vivat rex! Vivat rex!*"

He disappeared, still clamoring and raising his arms to the heavens. When he was in the street, the populace, who were swarming outside the Hôtel Saint-Pol, surrounded him and interrogated him, took sides for and against him, and lavished insults on the Duc d'Orléans, calling him a fratricide for having wanted to introduce his physician, a poisoner, to the king's bedside.

The clamors rose up, deafening and unintelligible, to the balcony on to which the Duc had followed Harsely and Rugiero, who were consulting the stars.

"What are those oafs shouting?" asked Orléans.

Instead of replying, the two physicians took him as a witness for what was happening in the heavens.

"Look, Monseigneur," cried Rugiero, triumphantly. "The Lion is in opposition to the Water-Carrier, by the distance of a throne, in the decadence of the Zodiac!"

"Master," retorted the Duc, preoccupied with the noise that he could hear, "look down below and not on high, and try to tell me what all those people in rumor want."

A formidable cry responded, dominating all the others:

"The king! The king! The king has been killed! Get the murderer! Get Louis d'Orléans!"

The astrologers, fearing projectiles, declared themselves satisfied with their celestial inspection and went to give their cares to the king, who was coming round without them.

"Mercy!" said Charles de Savoisy. "The people are seething. Monseigneur d'Orléans, go home in haste. The people are attacking, scaling the wall!"

"Infamy! But you all know that it was an accident and that I have nothing for which to reproach myself..."

"Do you think that they'll listen to your reasons?" said the queen, doubly anxious, quitting the endangered king for her imperiled lover. "Flee, hide for a few days."

"Flee? Me, hide? Never! Abandon my sick brother? Is it you, Madame, who is giving me such advice?"

"Am I not here to watch over the king?"

All of them cried: "Flee, prince, flee! Don't expose yourself to the brutality of the people!"

That unanimity might, perhaps have vanquished the duc, but Bourgogne, joining his somewhat ironic supplications to the general opinion, retained the prince.

"My brother, when he comes round," he said, "ought to see his brother, alive or dead, at his side. I'm staying, whatever happens."

A cry, dominating all the others, resounded like a summons: "The king! We want to see the king!"

The astrologers responded; "Thank God, he's opening his eyes!"

Alain Chartier ran to announce the good news to the people, but without success.

"They're lying!" clamored a tall, muscular fellow whose head had just emerged over the rim of the balcony.

Harsely came to Alain Chartier's aid.

"Yes, the king is saved, thanks to this constellated ring, with which I touched his forehead," he said, showing the sparkling ring.

"We'll believe it when we've seen the king himself," the fellow replied.

"What's that noise?" murmured Charles VI.

And with the aid of his astrologer, the queen and the Prince d'Orléans, the king succeeded in sitting up.

"Show us the king!" said the same man, in a comminatory tone. And he made as if to climb over the balustrade.

The people beating the wall down below were getting ready to climb up by means of the same asperities, bellowing: "The king! The king!"

That cry, prolonging through the air like the tolling of the great bell of the tower of Notre Dame, reverberated from chime to chime all the way to the eight new quarters that the latest edict of Charles VI had annexed to the enclosure of 1284 arpents composing Paris, commencing at the Rue Saint-Nicaise, traversing the present gardens of the Palais-Royal, following the alignment of the Fosses-Montmartre, Petit-Carreau and the direction of the old boulevards as far as the Arsenal, rallying all of the southern side of the Louvre to the Île Saint-Louis.

Paris counted no more than three hundred thousand inhabitants then, but it was quite enough for that population, agglomerated at a single point, to form a stormy sea of human heads rumbling with the cry: "We want to see the king!"

At such a moment, the thought could not come to any lord, even one as disdainful of the people as the Duc d'Orléans, to send soldiers again those dirty, ugly, ill-clad masses in order to beat them back. The popular wall would have fallen upon them and crushed them like insects. It was necessary to obey the crowd.

It was then that the Duc de Nevers, a prince beloved by the populace, advanced the proposition of answering that violent desire.

"Would it not be good, in order to calm the people of Paris, to bring the king to the window, if only for a few minutes?"

The uncles of Charles VI, who had recovered consciousness, begged him to address a few words to his faithful subjects.

"Worthy people!" groaned Charles VI. "I want to see them!"

As he struggled to get up, he was dressed in haste, and Nevers, aided by Orléans, carried him to the window.

"The king is alive!" cried the man stationed there.

He descended, or rather tumbled, into the street, still shouting: "The king is alive!"

An immense echoed repeated: "The king is alive!"

In the meantime, the king, sustained and shaking, said: "Hee hee! So I'm dead and buried! Hee hee! I'm damned like a miscreant. Oh what hell on earth! I've passed through the flames; there were six of us in the same furnace!"

"Let's get him away from the window," said Orléans, sadly. "Such a violent shock has disturbed his reason, and it's me..."

"By Jesus!" muttered Isabeau. "Duc, don't say that."

"Who speaks of Jesus among the damned? Oh how numerous they are in this plain of Hell!"

And the king extended his arms fearfully toward the crowd."

The crowd thought that he was blessing them.

"Get him away! Get him away!" repeated Orléans.

He was obeyed.

While the window was closed they were able to hear the populace shouting, singing and laughing, stopping in taverns to drink to the health of the resuscitated king.

The king had been placed in a large armchair with a Gothic back, in front of the hearth, where the fire had been reanimated, but at the sight of the flames, Charles VI stood up, leapt on to the armchair and remained standing there, like a statue on a pedestal, throwing of the pelisse that enveloped him, and as he still had a few extinct wisps of cotton about him, he said: "What have I done to be accursed? I'm already as hairy and horned as the devils. I have black claws and I feel the redness."

"Calm yourself, Sire," said Savoisy. "All your pain comes from the accident caused involuntarily by Monseigneur d'Orléans."

"Louis! Yes, it's Louis who has killed me for my crimes against my people! He's done well. I'm accursed."

"Mercy!" cried the witnesses. "The king, our master, has lost his reason!"

Everyone lowered his head. Isabeau hid hers in her hands, but she was thinking that, without a crime, she was about to seize her prey, to become regent, and that Nevers lay in wait for her like an obstacle to be overcome, which now threatened her ambition without threatening her felony.

"Who says that I've lost my reason?" cried Charles, in full delirium. "Mad? Me, the king? Is that possible? No, I don't want it. I want to dance."

He launched himself into the room, capering, breaking everything that came to hand. His physiognomy was red; he vomited blood; his eyes were bloodshot. It required the combined strength of the Duc d'Orléans and Nevers to contain him.

They carried him to the bed, where he collapsed, inundated with sweat. He slept there for twenty-four hours, under the guard of four vigorous men-at-arms and the two astrologer-physicians, who did not quit him.

The people continued to celebrate joyfully his return to health.

The next day, the dementia had not disappeared, but it was mild and punctuated by flashes of lucidity. One of those brief intervals sufficed for the queen to seize the opportunity to have herself awarded the presidency of the council. She also signed the commission of the Duc de Nevers for Hungary. It was only a flash, however; the king fell back into a species of idiocy, from which he never recovered completely.[26]

---

[26] History relates that it was not the fire in which he was burned that caused Charles VI's madness, which had commenced in August 1392 while he was passing through the forest of Le Mans with his army en route for Bretagne. Intermittent at first, however, the fits of dementia became more frequent after the fire. Previously nicknamed Charles le Bien-Aimé [Beloved], he was henceforth known as Charles le Fou [Mad].

VIII. THE OLD MANOR

The owls are heard fluttering in the rubble;
Goblins and winged dragons are ready for the Sabbat;
Around the old manor shades are seen wandering,
Hideous vampires are finishing their preparations.

The superstition and barbarity of the Middle Ages are astonishing not so much for their intensity as their duration. The Renaissance gilded the rut but did not fill it in.

Brantôme praised François I for having "made use of great pyres of protestants and showing the way with those salutary burnings." The very learned and very sage Duchâtel[27] believed in astrology, which he described as "A great art able to change the laws of nature and the worlds."

The Marquis de Saluces betrayed François I, whose friend he was, very handsomely recompensed for that service by Charles Quint, because a magician had predicted to him that it would be serving the cause of France. Catherine de Medicis did not provoke the Saint Bartholomew's Eve massacre in order to satisfy a vain cruelty; her amulets counseled her to do it. Louis XIV himself commanded dragoonings out of devotion, and redeemed his sins by his rigors.

In the fourteenth century, the spirit of darkness reigned as master. That is what emerges from the cruel and true scenes that are about to follow.

---

[27] The Breton military leader Tanneguy du Châtel (1369-1449)

Having said that, let is return to Aubert Le Flamenc, whom we left carrying his wife away. He summarizes his epoch. Two invisible fays, presiding over his birth, might have made him a man of intelligence or a fool. In becoming a soldier, he brought the intelligence and the stupidity into accord, without either being jealous of the other.

The son of a procurator at the Châtelet, he had quit the paternal office following an exploit that had nothing in common with the procedure. Mocked and jeered by the other clerks for his grotesque appearance, he had ended up felling one of them with a blow of his fist and had then fled into the depths of the province of Orléans, to the home of one of his aunts, who lived on the produce of a flock of goats and sheep, and who offered him the conduct of them.

Aubert, who had no choice, accepted, and the new pastor was intoxicated by solitude. Coiffed in a hood frayed by the wind and the rain, huddled in a fissure in a rock or under a clump of broom, he spent his days with his eyes lunged in the immensity, contemplating the clouds, admiring the strangeness and the variety of their forms. When dusk came, lying in the caravan from which he was supposed to be watching over his penned flock, he listened to the thousand nocturnal rumors and interpreted them. The moaning of the wind, the rumbling of thunder, the cries of owls, the howling of wolves were all, for Aubert, as many human voices, to which he lent the frame of a hectic drama, in which the Devil naturally played the leading role. That continual hallucination exhausted him. He was afraid of his own chimeras, and he decided one day to exchange the crook for the musket.

Does it not seem that Aubert Le Flamenc had the same vocation as Ignatius Loyola, mystic and soldier? In the soldiery he remained an illuminate. He would have made a warrior priest. You will see in due course why we are insisting on the religious side of the man, externally rude, but whose soul was, so to speak, always kneeling internally.

His marriage brought him back to superstitions, and after the humiliating ovation that he had been given in the court of France, the manor in which he took refuge with his wife exalted his fear of the demon and his furious recourse to Heaven.

The manor was nothing but an enfiefed ruin. It mostly consisted of huge damp rooms, cracked and covered in cobwebs, through which the dilapidated doors and unglazed windows allowed the wind to circulate in complete liberty. In one of the rooms the only furniture was a Gothic chair in worm-eaten wood, in which Aubert wrapped up Mariette as best he could, covering her with his own garments and drawing her near to the hearth, which he filled with a blazing fire.

Gradually, the bride warmed up, and Aubert recovered his composure.

In fleeing Paris on the same horse, with Mariette on the rump, the two spouses had stopped at the edge of the Bois de Vincennes at the Château de Beauté, to which the fief was related, and where the seneschal had delivered to the Sire de Cauny his letters of investiture.

They had also been able to hear a mass at the little church of Saint-Severin, contiguous with a monastery, in which Madame de Nevers was about to enter into a novena, in order to implore the success of the mission to Hungary.

That expedition, of which he had heard the news, was rolling around Aubert's head.

"Cordieu!" he had said to Mariette. "If your fortunate husband, Madame, didn't have better things to do, he would gladly have made war out there, in order to verify the dictum..."

"What dictum, Messire?" the wife had asked.

"It's said that when a Christian has cleaved a Saracen in two, all the devils in hell no longer have any purchase on him."

The Sire de Cauny's bravery, as is evident, was always lined with the fear of Satan.

While the couple talked before two blazing tree trunks, lackeys and vassals had assembled in order to welcome their new seigneur.

That population was preceded by a person of short stature, stiff, with a jaundiced complexion, whose paternal tone contrasted with his physiognomy; he was the bailiff. In spite of his appearance, he loved good wine, and the duty was imposed on him to drink in honor of Sire de Cauny.

"Do I have any wine?" asked Aubert Le Flamenc."

Some was procured for him very quickly; casks were rolled to the entrance of a adjoining room; victuals were brought, and the castellan had the pleasure of hearing the clamors that salute any advent. He felt a surge of pure pride. Decidedly, Monsieur d'Orléans was a great and good prince, and the bad joke of which Aubert Le Flamenc had been the victim was only an effect of the jealousy cited by his brilliant fortune.

Only one thing maintained melancholy in the mind of the new seigneur: the dilapidation of his manor.

He interrogated the bailiff. "These rooms haven't been inhabited for a long time, have they?"

"In fact, they have not been since the death of Messire Legorju fifteen years ago. As he had not left any

86

children, the fief was returned to the suzerain and remained without employment. Monsieur d'Orléans will doubtless give orders for it to be repaired, to have the crumbling walls rebuilt and the doors and windows replaced. That will certainly prevent the devils and witches from coming here to make their racket every night.

"What!" cried the colossus, with a fear that he could not dissimulate, and of which Mariette felt the reverberation.

"Are you sure of what you're saying, Master Bailiff?" she asked, shivering.

"Who would dare to doubt, Madame, that Monseigneur Satan holds his Sabbat every night in various places?"

"Oh, no one doubts it!" Aubert hastened to reply, fearing to be compromised toward Satan. "But that's not a reason for the Sabbat to be held here!"

"Alas, nothing is better known throughout the region, Messire. This manor has the same renown as the Clos Vauvert and the land of Mont-le-héry."

"True God! If that's the case we'll retake the road of Paris and await the restoration of this uninhabitable dwelling. But what does that serf in the livery of Monseigneur d'Orléans want? Has he come on the part of the seneschal to offer us the hospitality of the Château de Beauté?"

"Messire," said the newcomer, unrolling a parchment, "you are doubtless the castellan of the fief of Cauny?"

"I am."

"The messenger bowed and read: "By order of Monseigneur Louis de France, Duc d'Orléans, seigneur of the castellany of Beauté and its dependencies, Aubert Le Flamenc, his feudatory, is called to deliver the third part of the wine, meat and bread purchased by him to rejoice the men of his corps on the occasion of taking possession of his fief, a third part of which reverts by right to the suzerain."

"Is that the custom, Master Bailiff?" Aubert asked.

"It's the custom, and the custom made law in France."

"Then there's no reply to it?"

"No, it's as sacred as the tithe to the Church."

"It's just, you see, Bailiff, that I've never had a fief. I don't know the charges..."

"You have many others, in the quality of vavasour—which is to say, a vassal who has vassals. But on the other hand, you have the same rights over yours; that's a compensation."

"Ah! I have rights..."

"Yes, the rights of turbary, corvée, low justice and even a petty gibbet."

"A gibbet. That's precious, but I thought that since the harangue of the Chancellor of the University to Charles VI, our Sire, all those rights had been abolished?"

"For Paris, that's possible, but for the provinces, nothing of the sort. So, as I told you, you have the right to a petty gibbet. If a crime is committed on your land, you can require the hanging of the guilty party.

"Oh my God, what horror!" cried Mariette.

"Why, Madame? It does you honor in the eyes of people who traverse the land."

"You're a logician, Bailiff. In any case, if I do too much justice, Madame will claim her right to grant mercy."

The prince's messenger was waiting to be dismissed.

"That's good," said the Sire de Cauny, majestically. "It will be done as it is ordered." Then he turned to his lackeys: "Carry out the orders of Monseigneur d'Orléans."

IX. THE DROIT DU SEIGNEUR

"When such deeds are written in the law, they are qualified as rights; when the text of those laws is authentic and is produced, the officious role of negation becomes impossible."

People have always taken pleasure in cheating the revenue, so the lackeys and the vassals stole as much wine and meat as they delivered, and laughed heartily when their feints or concealments were discovered. That was all there was to it; everyone was amused.

No one was amused in the room where Aubert Le Flamenc, brave as he was, felt lugubrious sentiments assailing him at the approach of his wedding night, while Mariette thought too much about the Duc d'Orléans as the moment came only to think about her husband, and while the bailiff, looking at the bride and groom, thought about certain rights that Monseigneur could legally claim, not knowing that Monseigneur had claimed them far in advance.

"Master Bailiff," asked Sire de Cauny, "It's impossible to stay here tonight. Is there not some house that can be rented until tomorrow?"

"Impossible, Messire. There are only wretched hovels."

"It's necessary, them, that these people remain here to dance and rejoice until tomorrow—but two nights without sleep in very difficult, isn't that true, Madame?"

"I'll resign myself to it, Messire."

"But not me, my beautiful wife—for you are, and veritably, I haven't yet had time to perceive it. But here's another serf of the castellany. What can the other have forgotten?"

A second envoy, wearing the duc's livery, like the first, was in fact advancing, escorted by peasants who had scented some further incident.

Like the first, he unfurled a parchment, to which the seal of Monseigneur d'Orléans was appended, and after having bowed respectfully he read in an imposing voice:

"By order of Monseigneur Louis de France, Duc d'Orléans, suzerain of the Castellany of Beauté and its dependencies, Aubert Le Flamenc, his feudatory for the fief of Cauny, is summoned to send to the Château de Beauté immediately, Mariette d'Anghuien, whom he married under the auspices of Monseigneur d'Orléans, in order to acquit the right of prelibation, as is customary."

"Head and blood!" cried Aubert. "You're lying!"

"I have not lied; I have delivered my message."

Mariette had recoiled in fear.

"Monseigneur is incapable of such villainy," said Aubert.

"Permit me, Messire," said the bailiff, with a magisterial gesture, "to say that such words are inappropriate. This is a custom as old as the monarchy; you have the same right over your vassals...that is a compensation."

"No, no, it cannot—and then, the duc isn't at the château...it's an infamy of the seneschal."

"Monseigneur is not at the château, that it true...but he will be tomorrow," riposted the serf, emboldened by the presence of the bailiff.

"And it's by his order that you have come?"

"By order of Monseigneur. Here is his seal; here are his arms."

Aubert took the parchment, tore it up, but it, trampled it underfoot and struck the serf in the face.

"Take this to him!" he cried, throwing the pieces in his face.

"It's easy for you to strike a poor serf like me, who is doing his duty; but Messire the Seneschal is on my heels; he will certify what I say."

"By my patron saint, let him come. Have no fear, Madame."

"Messire," murmured Mariette, in a tremulous voice, "Don't expose yourself to such danger... promise... pretend to consent."

"Have no fear, Madame! Vassals, you owe me obedience. I'm counting on you."

The villeins, warmed by the wine and intoxicated by the fine bearing of their seigneur, responded with enthusiasm: "Yes, yes!"

"Uh oh," muttered the bailiff. "this is rebellion!" After having looked out of the window, he added: "Messire, believe me, submit. There's only just time. Here's the seneschal, with a troop of archers."

"Me, submit! Never." And, turning toward his vassals: "Hola, my friends, which of you have the courage to put yourselves in the service of their lord and master? Have at the seneschal! Have at the thief of honor!"

"Yes, yes, out with the seneschal!" brayed a few drunken voices. The greater number hesitated and shut up, chilled by the sight of the seneschal, who penetrated into the manor.

"Now, my archers," said the seneschal to his escort. "There's no need here of blades or arrows; unstring your bows and your lances, and only strike with the wood those villeins that are drunk, on my word."

At that soldierly injunction, voices from the group of goatherds, cowherds and field-laborers were heard to say: "Hey, Master Seneschal, I'm not one of them."

And the echoes of the hall repeated: "Nor me! Nor me!"

"Ah! There's your valor a little sobered up, my knights. So deliver the vassale immediately, in accordance with the custom."

Aubert enveloped Mariette's waist with his left hand and, brandishing his sword, said to the Seneschal: "Come and get her!"

"Messire Aubert, this is a great treason," replied the seneschal, with a fine sang-froid. "The husband who rebels against a right as ancient and as just is, in accordance with the ancient usages, apprehended bodily, dragged into the courtyard of the seigneurial château, attached to a stake and delivered to his suzerain's dog pack, to be torn apart.

"And you think that just?" replied Aubert, furiously. "Since you're alive, it's because you've passed through it."

The seneschal did not reply; it was the bailiff who intervened, doctorally. "This right has been in the law since the earliest times of the monarchy; even ecclesiastical seigneurs can exercise it; but they abstain and receive in exchange a gift in *écus de soleil*, qualified as the right of Lord God. And when a married villein settles outside the villeiny of a fief, the lord thus losing his nuptial right, the vassal is obliged to pay his seigneur three sols in compensation. *Cum villanus maritat filiam suam extra villanagium, debet tres solides de culagio...*"

The bailiff was threatening to reel off a long chaplet of texts, but the seneschal's patience had run out. Seeing that, the serf who had brought the second missive of the Duc d'Orléans cut off the speech of the man of law.

"Messire," he said to the Sire de Cauny, "I am the keeper of Monseigneur's pack… it's me who will be forced to launch them against you. Spare me that dolor."

A scornful smile was Aubert's response.

"Let's go, bumpkins," cried the seneschal. "It's the last summons. Either the wife is handed over by you, or I'll exercise against the village the right of seizure reestablished by Monseigneur le Duc d'Orléans in your favor, and in addition, I'll marry a few of you to Madame la Hart."[28]

"The right of seizure!" repeated the terrified villeins, sensible above all to the penalty. And as if they were running to defend her, thy hurled themselves at Mariette in order to seize her—but the frightful windmill that Aubert executed with his sword made them recoil.

Then the seneschal gave his archers the order to fall upon the rebel. One of the most agile attempted to leap upon his shoulders in order to hamper his movement, but he fell back, eviscerated. A second who came to the rescue received a blow on the head that split it; a third, his throat slashed, fell on his two companions, but a fourth succeeded in dislodging Aubert from the chimney-breast, against which he had braced himself, and forced him back against the wall. Aubert was obliged momentarily to detach his left arm from Mariette's waist in order to seize the archer he was threatening with his sword; Mariette slid to the ground and fainted. Aubert stepped over her, seized the archer, strangled him and threw him at the seneschal.

That superb resistance caused the opinion of the serfs to swerve again. They liked strength; they did not like archers; perhaps they were about to give reinforce-

---

[28] i.e. the gallows.

ment to their seigneur and acclaim the Sire de Cauny when the latter, wanting to protect Mariette better, cleaved forward. Unfortunately, he slipped in the blood that moistened the paving stones, could not retain his balance, and, fearing to fall on the recumbent Mariette, he threw himself sideways and fell alongside her

Once on the ground he could not get up again. Surrounded, seized and tied up in bonds that cut into his flesh, he could only howl: "To me, my friends, help me! Kill me! Kill me, then!"

Mariette was carried away unconscious; the serfs, no longer daring to choose, followed the archers, and the bailiff, left almost alone with the dead, the wounded and the Sure de Cauny, said to him paternally: "Messire, I'm confused for you. I don't know how Monseigneur will envisage your unqualifiable resistance to an immemorial usage. You cannot argue ignorance. In consenting to become his feudatory, you knew the charges that would weigh upon you as vavasour. It was open to you to decline the offer of the fief of Cauny. Blood has been shed; you have wounded several archers representing the seigneurial authority. You will have to respond for this rebellion before the High Bailiff of Nogent."

The seneschal was standing on the threshold, He had his turn.

"The vassale is in my power," he said, "my mission is concluded. As for you, villeins who have reentered into duty, I will grant you grace of the right of seizure and content myself with a tax of twenty gold sous; but I demand that that gold has the effigy of Charles V, gold of this reign only being worth half as much because of the alloy practiced under the minority of our Sire. I have spoken."

He remounted his horse and rode away.

"Twenty gold sous!" cried the peasants, tearfully. "But that's our ruination!"

"God alive!" vociferated Aubert, appealing to his vassals. Have you no wives, daughters, sisters? Who are you, then, cowards, sons of jacques? Is it money that you need. Rummage in my satchel, take it for the expenses of war, for we're going to take the Château de Beauté! Let's go! Untie me; I'll arm you, we'll depart...

"Alas," added the Sire de Cauny, looking around him, "they've departed without me; but it's not to avenge me!"

Desperate, he was struggling in vain against his bonds when a little shepherd huddled in a corner approached him compassionately.

"Not everyone has gone, Messire," he said in a low voice.

"Who are you?"

"One of your shepherds."

"Do you have a knife?"

"Yes." And the shepherd cut the ropes binding the colossus.

When the latter was on his feet, the shepherd, addressing a former shepherd, said: "Messire, if I dared to give you some advice..."

"Speak."

"I would recommend you to make a circle round yourself three times and cry: 'Monseigneur Satan, I request you to come to my aid.' He'll come."

The superstitious Aubert shook his head; he found the advice good, but he said in his fury, holding out his clenched fist: "I am Satan, and I shall wreak a terrible revenge."

The little shepherd did not wait to be thanked; he was afraid, and he escaped.

X. MASTER GONIN

'Tis midnight, witch; bestride your broom.
They're all assembled, out there under the great orb,
Satan is with them, mounting his enormous ram.

Aubert Le Flamenc, steady on his feet again, pushed a door and, after having parted a thick curtain of cobwebs, penetrated into a room whose windows, still entire, intercepted the air that entered freely elsewhere and maintained a strong odor of mildew. Although the windows were intact, they were covered by a layer of dust that daylight could not traverse. Aubert, superstitious as we know him to be, felt ill at ease in the midst of an obscurity aggravated by a suffocating odor. So brave a little while ago, the colossus was trembling like a child. Shadows passed before his frightened eyes, putting on various forms. At one moment, he thought he perceived Mariette and the seneschal. Then he ran to seize the former and strike the latter, but he only attained emptiness. In his rage, she caused a door to fly apart in splinters, and through that exit he arrived in the great hall, the former hall of vassals, where he thought he respired an odor of sulfur that could only be the atmosphere of the Sabbat.

"Oh!" he murmured, terrified. Then, abruptly, he added: "Well, if I'm to see Satan, I'll ask him for my vengeance. No more of these terrors, unworthy of me. I'll give my soul for the life of that infamous duc! The wretch! Perhaps he's hugging my beautiful Mariette in his arms. Let's go! No recoiling."

He traced the fateful circle around himself with his sword and pronounced, in a tremulous voice: "Monseigneur Satan, I request that you come to my aid!"

Then he listened; his ears were buzzing, but no distinct sound responded to him.

"However," he murmured, "It's certain that Hell hears all imprecations, as Heaven hears all prayers."

He took few steps, shaking with anger, his legs unsteady, and he repeated, in a louder voice: "Monseigneur Satan, I request you to come to my aid!"

Suddenly—O prodigy!—it seemed to him that a light, a follet, shone in the distance.

Can that, he said to himself, as his teeth chattered, *be the diamond that Satan bears in his forehead?*

Almost immediately, he heard an evidently infernal dialogue.

"Is the Mouth of Hell open wide?" asked a cavernous voice.

"Yes, Master," replied another voice, no less sepulchral.

"And the furnace of the damned?"

"It is ardent and profound; all the husbands in Hell could enter it without filling it."

That allusion to his conjugal woes might have made him suspicious, but Aubert was not astonished that Hell already knew his tortures.

Cold sweat pearled on his brow.

Then he saw vague, strange forms moving toward him. They really were the hideous phantoms, such as the likes of Lancre, Leloyer[29] and other celebrated

---

[29] Pierre de Lancre, author of *Tableau de l'inconstance des mauvais anges et démons* (1612) and Pierre Le Loyer, author of *Discours et histoires des spectres, visions et apparitions des*

demonographers of the fifteenth century depicted the counselors of Satan: two horns at the neck, another on the forehead, bristling hair, a pale face, round and blazing eyes; a goat's beard, similar hands and feet, pointed and armed with talons, resembling the claw of a bird of prey, and finally, as a complement, the tail of a donkey. Such was the aspect of the principal demons that appeared.

My blood is running cold! Aubert said to himself. Then, stimulating himself, he said: *Think of your wife, wretched coward!* And, rage rendering him courage, he cried again:

"Monseigneur Satan, I request you to come to my aid!"

To begin with, there was a profound silence; then there was a murmur, which augmented and ended up bursting into sonorous diabolical laughter

This is a somewhat clownish Sabbat! Aubert thought.

While he gazed at Satan's band, a horned and bearded demon who had slipped behind him came around him to take a stance in front of him. He was folded upon himself in a parcel, like a man devoid of legs, but gradually he unwound, stood up, grew, all black, and demanded: "Who calls me? Is it you, profane?"

"It's me," replied Aubert Le Flamenc, who did not flinch.

The Devil seemed far more astonished than the man who evoked him, for, at the risk of giving himself away, he murmured, with a slight snigger: "Oho! A pleasant

---

esprits, anges, démons et âmes se montrant visibles aux hommes (c.1695).

adventure! Here's an encounter that abridges my task; it's only to me, Gonin, that such things happen!"

"Damn! Hell is more cheerful than it's rumored, from what I can see," said poor Aubert, vexed by that snigger.

Recalled to the dignity of his role, the Devil held himself magisterially and said in a voice that seemed to emerge from a tomb: "You're speaking loudly, friend, so you're afraid. Don't worry. Between horned folk, confidence is required. I've come without a whirlwind of flames; speak to me as to a mortal. What do you want?"

"Oh, Monseigneur, is it necessary to confide my shame to you? You made allusion to it yourself..."

Aubert touched his forehead.

"Yes, yes, I know. Louis d'Orléans has enabled you to marry a woman of high rank, for which marriage a charivari was held at the court...."

"Yes, yes... that's enough."

"The same Louis d'Orléans has just had your wife abducted, in order that she can keep him company at the Château de Beauté, where he will reside for a few days. What do you want?"

"I want my wife."

"Good."

"I want to avenge myself, to kill the abductor. I want Hell to make me all the advances possible on my future damnation."

"You're asking a lot for very little. Your damnation, you say? I'd lose by it. The Duc d'Orléans is damning half of France; I have fine plans for him. And then, he's a devoted prince, although licentious. He carries on his person one of the ribs of Saint Denys, which his brother gave him. I can't do anything against that defense. Let's finish it. I'll render your wife to you."

"Nothing but that? What do you want in return? Is that sufficient to doom my soul?"

"Who said anything about your soul? Take your wife; I only impose one condition: that you flee with her as far as you can, and make sure that she never sees the Duc d'Orléans again."

"Oh, by death! Have no doubt of that; but time is pressing."

"Oh, yes, poor man; follow me, then."

"On foot?"

"No, in a cart with my devils, who are good devils."

"But I thought a word was sufficient for you to transport us down below, or to bring my wife here."

"Old worn-out means. Hell only employs natural means henceforth. Follow me."

Sire de Cauny followed him, but he said, mentally: *It's singular that Monseigneur Satan walks like me, and doesn't reek of wax or sulfur. But what does it matter, if he keeps his promise?*

It is thus that incredulity is born in souls, when they sense the necessity of being grateful for an act of faith.

XI. MARGUERITE DE HAINAUT

She was beautiful, with her queenly step,
Her soft voice charmed like a siren song;
She was beautiful, young, and mad for pleasure,
And her blue eyes brooded unslakable desires.

Between the Bois de Vincennes and the small town of Nogent, about half an hour from either, the mass of the Château de Beauté launched forth like a standing giant, with thick gray walls.

A high tower, built in the times of feudal discords, surmounted by a rounded block of stone, resembled the arm of the giant, lifting a heavy cannonball above his head, ready to crush any imprudent enemy who advanced that far. A sold surrounding wall circled the crenellated base, which was tailored to the four horizons. Narrow loopholes gaped around it like the eyes of birds of prey. The approaches to it were defended by a ditch as wide as it was deep, but the drawbridge was only lowered in the presence of the prince. A postern led into open country by way of a tunnel, the issue of which was lost in the middle of a thicket of thorny bushes.

The Duchesse de Nevers had been initiated into the mysterious vicinity of that postern and she opened it with the little golden key that Orléans had given her, when she wanted to break off the religious practices of the convent of Saint-Saturnin, to which she sometimes retired. That convent was situated some distance from the château. It contained uncloistered nuns, whom grand dames in a humor for novenas came to join and who diversified their games, in the example of the duchesse.

That monastery was a true mill; one entered or left it at will. It was also a veritable house of pleasure. The Bois de Vincennes was simultaneously appropriate to an amorous redoubt and a hunting lodge. The boisterous penitents loved to beat the country in autumn, mounted on a sprightly charger with a falcon on the wrist, which they released placidly against the gentle skylarks soaring and whistling in the sky.

From the top of the tower dominating the Château de Beauté, a hunter, who was none other than the Duc d'Orléans, watched from time to time the huntress Dianas riding, and launched toward the most beautiful in the guise of a gerfalcon, a varlet who held the employment, with velvet claws, who brought back via the tunnel the lovely bird-catcher turned prey, who did not struggle overmuch.

The interior of the château was disposed like all the manors of the epoch, but the rooms were better furnished and ornamented by certain artistic curiosities of which the prince was a lover.

In addition to its rich furniture, the room into which we shall penetrate in order to describe it, not as wide as it was long, but vast enough to fold a banquet there for a hundred knights, was ornamented by a full-length portrait of the queen, Isabeau de Bavière, painted on glass by Jehan de Muret. She was represented during her entry to Paris—on 20 August 1389, according to Froissart—at the moment when the most gracious and the best made of the troupe of the Prince of Fools, clad, says Juvénal des Ursins, in the guise of an angel, "came by means of well-made engines from the towers of Notre Dame and put a beautiful crown on her head."

In the background, the people were visible, kept at a distance, and in the middle of the crowd, two men on the same horse, prevented from advancing by sergeants armed with long staffs, striking the men and the horse indistinctly. The two riders were the king and Savoisy. Charles VI had said to his chamberlain: "I beg you, Savoisy, as much as I can, to mount a good horse, and I will climb up behind you, and we shall dress so that no one will recognize us, and go to see my wife's entry.

Savoisy, spurred by the king, hastened in his turn to spur the horse; but the sergeants, "who did not know either the king or the chamberlain, struck them with their staves, giving the king several well-landed blows, and in the evening, at the court, the thing was known and recited, and people began to laugh at it, and the king laughed at it himself."

Charles VI wanted the painter to reproduce with his brush a scene that had amused him, although bruised. In principle, the Château de Beauté had belonged to the queen. Later, she had made a gift of it to the Duc d'Orléans, without suspecting, of course, the gallant destination for which he reserved it. As an entrance to the game, he had had the aforementioned tunnel excavated.

Now, in the hall known as the Knights' chamber, on a bed of repose, a young woman was asleep, her slumber agitated by feverish dreams. At times she seemed to wake up, bounding on the bed, but after a few minutes of collapse, she resumed her troubled sleep.

Suddenly, the painting representing Isabeau's entry, which masked a door, rotated on itself and gave passage to an aerial form. It closed immediately over the issue that it covered with the width of its frame, with no more noise than a butterfly makes giving a kiss to a rose.

She was an adorable creature, with a slender and supple waist. Nothing more gracious than that beloved body. The hair, of a strange blonde, sometimes allowed the sight, under jets of pale light, streaks of fire and gold that delighted and fascinated the eyes. Her skin, of a mat whiteness, was so delicate that the slightest veins fled there in networks of transparent blue. It was like a surface of azure and alabaster that no wrinkle furrowed and no cloud striped. The cheeks had a velvet respected by the fatigues of a course through the fields, which the beating of the heart and the agitation of the bosom indicated sufficiently. The pallor of the arms was admirable. The woman attested the triumph of an omnipotent chisel, a masterpiece of the divine artist.

The eyes of Marguerite de Hainaut, Duchesse de Nevers—for it was her—seemed the masterpiece of that masterpiece. Picture long lashes curved back, lowering over velvet and flame. Their expression had an indescribable mixture of chastity and sensuality, a rare and precious assemblage. When a smile illuminated them, flashes of sensibility and pleasure sprang forth. The well-designed mouth, the sensual lips with the brightness and the freshness of a rose, opened over even pearls, well-arranged and so white as to give the desire to be bittern by them until blood flowed. As for the hands, Orléans put himself on his knees in order to kiss them.

So much for the mortal envelope; the soul it imprisoned was no less beautiful and no less loving than the pagan Venus.

That woman would have been the perfect wife and mother, if ironic fatality had not given her Jean de Nevers for a husband and Louis d'Orléans for a lover.

After a moment of breathlessness demanded by the journey from the convent of Saint-Saturnin, where she was on novena, to the Château de Beauté, she murmured in a low voice: "Finally, I've been able to arrive without accident!"

Groping around, she encountered a chair, on which she allowed herself to collapse, and she abandoned herself to her reflections.

Her amour was the principal, radiant subject; fears enveloped it like a cloud, but did not stifle it.

She thought about Louis. Why was he not there? She thought that she heard a sigh. *I'm mad*, she thought. However, she listened, and a further sound caused her to tremble.

Could the astrologer Coquerel be right? she wondered. *Do spirits that love one another come together before the bodies?*

Immediately, the sigh was accentuated and Marguerite heard, distinctly: "Monseigneur, for pity's sake let me go."

Someone here! A woman, a rival!

Marguerite stood up, quivering and advanced toward the sound.

A beam of crepuscular light had just traversed the room.

"Alone, defenseless!" the unknown woman continued to groan.

She's dreaming! What is she saying? thought the duchesse.

"Was the virgin not enough? Must you have the wife?" And, struggling, the recumbent woman added: "No, no! Never!"

"That's not a rival," murmured Marguerite, with a smile.

The unknown woman had woken up; she was trying to emerge from the nightmare that still enveloped her.

"What a frightful dream!" she said. "Where am I?"

"You're in a trap from which I want to extract you," said the duchesse, advancing and raising her voice.

"You! Who are you?"

"A woman who feels sorry for you."

"A woman who wants to free me? Perhaps it's you who have put me in his arms!"

"You're mad! We have no time to lose. It will soon be daylight. You're in the duc's house; he's going to come. Do you want to wait?"

"But what proof do I have...?"

"If I wanted to deliver you to him, I would only have to leave you where he has had you placed."

Instinctively, Mariette d'Anghuien, hallucinated by the narcotic that was slowly dissipating, tried to flee. Marguerite stopped her, holding both her hands forcefully, and with a few rapid, energetic words succeeded in persuading her, or at least in overcoming her resistance.

She drew her toward the issue that was veiled by the painting. As she was about to press the secret spring, however, she heard a key grate in a lock. Then she pushed Mariette into a lateral cabinet, recommending her to remain still there until she could escape through the door hidden behind the painting. Then the duchesse threw herself on to the bed where the unconscious Mariette had been thrown, and pretended to be asleep.

Scarcely had she adopted that posture than the seneschal, followed by a varlet and a man-at-arms, came to inform the person that he believed to be Aubert Le Flamenc's wife that she had to accompany him to the prince, who was waiting for her.

The order had been given in a respectful tone, but it was an order nevertheless.

Marguerite obeyed it meekly, and as she had drawn down her veil to hide her shame, the seneschal did not perceive the substitution.

Unfortunately for Mariette, the varlet and the man-at-arms, who addressed one another as Humbert and Riblet, remained in the room. Humbert lit a big fire; then they both sat down at the table and began a game of dice, in order to kill time like good companions.

XII. THE OLD GOAT'S HORN

Horns on the head, tail erect,
And not feeling the heat;
As a monk, but a stupid monk
Satan presents himself—to do what?

The sun has finished inundating with light the room that the duchesse and the seneschal have just quit; now we can describe it. It is exceptionally ornate. The ogival windows have panes that wooden lattices frame like lace. The ceiling has arabesques and little painted amours, of a rather mediocre execution.

The walls of the banqueting hall are lined with fleurs-de-lys in very thin copper; chairs with high backs advance their arms, with tabourets and woolen cushions embroidered with flowers. A lectern supports a vast folio manuscript of prayers, all written on parchment by the hand of the chancellor of the University. That lectern, as well as a table in tropical hardwood, is the work Michel Bourdin, one of the most skillful sculptors of the thirteenth century.[30]

On the table was a strange literary accumulation. A canticle to the Virgin was juxtaposed with a more profane song to Madame Venus. The *Imitatio Christi* sustained a ballad by the poet Cretin. The best place was given to the works of Alain Charier, among others the *Quadrilogue*, strangely humanitarian poetry in which the

---

[30] A blatant anachronism; the sculptor Michel Bourdin lived in the seventeenth century, as did Guillaume Cretin, the poet cited subsequently.

nobility, the clergy and France were placed in regard to the people, protesting against abuses. The Duc d'Orléans used the pretext of that book to call Alain Chartier "Thévenin the Second," making allusion to the fool of Charles V, his father.[31]

Other manuscripts would furnish us with a commencement of a catalogue of the Duc d'Orléans' library, but the list would be too long.

After three games of dice, the varlet, bled dry, parted company with the victor and went to blow the fire, which was threatening to go out, while the man-at-arms got to his feet and made a tour of the room, inspecting all the nooks and pausing in the four corners, as if in search of the definition of the square on the hypotenuse. He stopped for a long time before the painting of the entry of Isabeau de Bavière and admired the fine bearing of his sovereign loudly; then he shook his head, as if a philosophical thought had just crossed his mind.

"What's given you that surly expression all of a sudden?" asked Humbert.

"Don't you find," Riblet replied, "that Madame Isabeau is pulling a face at the moment?"

"Bah! If that ray of sunlight over there turned toward her lovely face, you'd see her smile."

"Hmm, friend. I maintain that in spite of the sun, she'd have the same expression. Between us, it's because she has no reason to be content."

"Why?"

"Madame la Reine hasn't generously made a gift of this château to Monseigneur d'Orléans for him to do…what we see."

---

[31] Charles V's fool Thévenin de St. Leger, who died in 1374, is known to history by virtue of his tomb at Senlis,

"Well, yes... but what does it matter?"

"Feign ignorance then—as if in such adventures the people of the household aren't always the first to be instructed, before society and the husbands...when the later succeed in being instructed."

"And when they're husbands for good."

"I tell you, I who am from Monseigneur d'Orléans' town house and who arrived with him from Paris, that if Madame la Reine knew what is happening here, she'd come at the gallop of her white hackney, throw the vassale out and have Monseigneur before her like a scholar at the Sorbonne. Oh, I've seen that, I who am speaking; I've seen it."

"Me too, friend, since it's necessary to say something to pass the time."

"Good, what have you seen?"

"When Monseigneur and Madame Isabeau came to repose here from the hunt in the Bois de Vincennes last summer, there were still young women from Nogent, from the fiefs of Moineaux, Cauny and Perreux at the entrance to the château, who had brought baskets of flowers and fruits. And Monseigneur d'Orléans often took them by the chin: 'Oh, my darling, how dainty and becoming you are! When will you be married? I'll take care to be at the château that day!"

"Really? And the queen?"

"The queen said to them, angrily: 'Get out of here, little whores, or sluts; stop pestering my pages and varlets.'"

"It was in the interest of morals, then?"

"Yes, yes, not for anything else—but enough laughter. I can hear the seneschal coming back!"

Riblet went to stand guard near the main door, while Humbert attended to his function of varlet, seeming to be busy, agitating in the guise of dusting the furniture.

He was just in time; the seneschal did indeed arrive with a heavy and measured tread. He made a gesture to Humbert and the latter brought a chair closer to the fire; the seneschal say down, sank into it and delivered himself to a profound meditation. Since Monseigneur was going to spent a few days at the château, how should he be amused?

The seneschal poked the fire and made flames spring up from the log. Poking a fire relieves, amuses and stimulates ideas. Now, the seneschal was, precisely, in search of an idea. He poked and poked, with unequivocal gestures of impatience, annoyed by not being able to catch an idea, a midge that sometimes becomes an eagle.

As everything wearies, however, even searching for ideas, the seneschal stopped poking. Then, stretching his limbs like a cat, his eyes half-closed, he gazed vaguely at the red furnace accumulated under the log. Suddenly, the half-consumed log cracked, broke, rolled a little, and formed by its outline a pointed rock. It seemed to the seneschal that on the summit of that ardent rock he saw gallows dancing. The gibbets were agitating their long arms rhythmically, swinging skeletons.

They were not visions of ideas, they were a depiction of his functions. The seneschal's ill humor increased, and, turning toward Riblet, as if the latter were about to give him a pretext for hanging, he said: "Man-at arms! Hold your sword neither straight nor erect, the point toward the groin, in the right hand, thumb to the left, in order that..."

He was interrupted by the sound of a hunting horn.

"Who is sounding at the château? What does that old goat's horn want? Riblet, send four of your men to the loopholes to see what miscreant has just scratched my ears."

"Yes Messire."

"And have him hanged if he does it again!"

"Yes, Messire."

At that point, however, the horn played a tune. Riblet did not leave; he beat time from head to foot; the man-at-arms was a melomaniac.

"Oho! He's a practiced player. Riblet, go where I told you, and send me the watchman."

"I'm going, Messire. As for the watchman, I can see him coming down from his station and coming this way."

From the threshold, Riblet hailed the watchman, and then drew away.

The seneschal, who had come to his feet with a single bound on hearing the sound of the horn, to the extent that his corpulence permitted him to bound—for it is necessary to picture a sort of Silenus with a salt-and-pepper beard, having never had on his chubby face any trace of worries or wrinkles, only a few fan-like creases formed in the fat—settled down in his chair again at his post beside the hearth, his hands joined blissfully over his abdomen, and waited for the watchman, who did not take long to appear.

"What news, watchman?" he asked.

"Messire, it's a troupe of minstrels requesting hospitality at the castellany.

"Minstrels! Oho! That's an idea. Let one come in as a specimen, and if he has the appearance of a good fellow, they'll be welcome. Monseigneur likes such folk, although they're vulgar clowns, for the most part, except for the Fraternity of the Passion, who are said to be honest persons exercising their art for the glory of God.[32] Go, watchman, go, introduce one—only one."

"Yes, Messire, but I believe they're the Fraternity of the Passion, for they're hooded like monks."

"We'll see! Go."

When the watchman had disappeared from the garden, he traversed the first courtyard, passed under an arcade in the Norman style, and then opened a door lined with iron, capable of resisting the most violent attacks, which gave entry to another courtyard closed by buildings, including the chapel. Then he went along the wall to the south-western corner, where there was a round and obscure opening leading to the men-at-arms' stairway, connected to the subterranean stairway to the dungeons, from which one rarely emerged. The watchman went down again on the side opposite the guard-room, and soon found himself in the lodge of the guardian of the drawbridge.

The drawbridge was lowered, on the seneschal's order, and raised again after having let in a minstrel. Under the conduct of the watchman, the latter passed through the places we have just described, darting an observant gaze into all the corners and turnings he trav-

---

[32] The *Confrérie de la Passion* [Fraternity of the Passion] was a company of amateur actors drawn from the bourgeoisie of Paris, who were given a license by Charles VI in 1402 to produce mystery plays based on the scriptures, which rapidly became popular. Such plays had originally been performed in churches by monks, but a papal bull of 1210 forbidding clergy to perform in public had resulted in their organization being taken over by town guilds.

ersed, storing them in his memory, as a skillful captain studies the field and terrain of a military action.

A lush and leafy boscage, irrigated by jets of water—an April meadow, even though it was February—gave the castle a cheerful and agreeable aspect on that side. Although it had been built in the same epoch as the Hôtel Saint-Pol, the Château de Beauté was better embellished than the palace near the Bastille. It was fleuronned, blazoned, flanked with pretty turrets, decorated with arabesques, equipped with balconies all the way to the top, with flags and poles.

In the middle of the "April meadow" stood a fountain representing the three Graces, as Louis d'Orléans loved them; that group, by an Italian whose name has not reached us, was only a copy of the Greek group, but well executed.

The banqueting hall was on the ground floor overlooking the garden. We can complete the summary description we have given of it. Silver trays, candelabras, amphorae of Venetian crystal encrusted with lapis and topaz, ebony sideboards, silver goblets, cups sculpted on designs by Florentine artists, silky fabrics and carpets brought from Persia by knights returned from the Orient embellished and garnished the great hall.

Our minstrel, or Brother of the Passion, as the watchman called him indistinctly, traversed the garden, preparing his eyes to admire the marvel of the château, the beautiful hall that had doubtless been designated to him as the central point of his operations. It was there that the suzerain assembled his vassals and vavasours on certain days, and made good cheer to the light of torches held by the prettiest vassals, semi-clad. It was there that the minstrels sang their ballads.

In the time of the present proprietor, they took are only to sing the productions of the princely poet, who was treated as the foremost poet of France. The Duc d'Orléans was sensible to that flattery.

The hall was twenty-four paces long and thirty broad. The glance that the monk darted at it when he entered appeared to satisfy him. His arms folded over his breast, his head bowed, his stance humble and his voice halting, he advanced toward the seneschal, who stood up to receive him.

The monk's robe produces its effect, whoever the monk might be.

"May the great Saint Julien and the other saints preserve you from all evil, Messire," said the monk.

"Let him also aid you, Master," replied the fat man.

"Would it please you to permit a few Brothers of the Passion to spend the day and the following night in the castellany? We have a great need to repose and to repair our cart, the wheels of which are broken. We were counting on continuing our route and reaching Paris this evening, but the thaw has made a sea of mud and we would only emerge from the Bois de Vincennes crippled, it's so wet. We're poor Christians, Messire, and peaceful folk. We'll pay for our food, if necessary."

"Ha ha! In ringing and shiny coin known to the eyes and ears alone. Well, sit down... Humbert, bring a chair to the other side of the hearth. As for you, watchman, return to your post."

The watchman saluted and left. The valet brought forward the chair, on which the minstrel sat down, after which the seneschal plunged into his own like a lap-dog curling up.

Humbert closed the door at the back, next to which he remained, awaiting the orders that it pleased the seneschal to give—which did not take long. Can one chat without drinking?

XIII. THE FRATERNITY OF THE PASSION

In a monstrous décor deploy the richness
Of a frightful scene pressed in the frame.

The seneschal allowed his guest to warm himself, of which he seemed to have need, and in the meantime, he made a sign to the varlet to bring a cup of hypocras with musk and amber; but the minstrel preferred a horn of spiced wine.

After a double swig, the seneschal clicked his tongue and said: "Now, where have you come from, my guest, and why are you en route?"

"We've come from Bordeaux in Guyenne, Messire. Having learned that the king, by letters patent of December last, had authorized the representation in Paris of the Mysteries that have so far only been played in the provinces, we set forth for such a great city, which counts more than three hundred thousand souls, where we hope to earn our living honorably, above all by novelty."

Oh, I say all my prayers for the success of the Fraternity of the Passion, whom I esteem particularly among the folk of their estate. But there's a rival to dread in Paris."

"To dread?" said the minstrel, adjusting his hood as if he had felt a draught in his face.

"So it's said, for I don't know him, never having seen him, but it's said that he's an astonishing comedian."

The minstrel uncovered his head completely.

"What do you call him?" he asked.

"The Prince of Fools, the leader of a troupe of 'Carefree Children,' who have been playing farces and satires for two years in the markets of Paris, with the protection of the king and the queen."

"Ah! You mean Master Gonin, a great braggart, who has the pretention of having invented satirical farces; which brings a great prejudice to our Mysteries, because the populace, in France, would rather laugh than weep. This Gonin also claims to be changing farces into comedies, as in the time of the Greeks and Romans, those pagans who had no knowledge of the beauties of Christianity. He's a great rogue whom it's necessary to take to hang at Montfaucon. He's recruited his troupe, whom he calls comedians, among the rogues, vagabonds and bad lots of the great city, who swarm in the Court of Miracles. But can one compare those buffooneries to the noble and religious spectacle of our mysteries, which last for several days and employ no less than three hundred characters?"

The minstrel's voice lingered over the number three hundred.

"Good God! Are your companions in such number at the gate of the château?"

"Oh, no, Messire, unfortunately"

"Very fortunately, on the contrary. Damn! Three hundred! That would be enough to consume the provisions of the château in a single day. We only have twelve or fifteen men-at-arms here. By the way, Humbert, go and ask how our five wounded men are doing. Come back and give me a report.

While the varlet went out, the minstrel agitated his fingers slowly, with a smile, as if he were counting, to subtract five from fifteen.

The seneschal went on: "How many are you?"

"We're only the residue of a much more considerable troupe, only fifteen, but in Paris we'll join brethren who have already arrived."

"I've had an idea, Master. Monseigneur Louis d'Orléans is presently at the château, and you might have the honor of appearing before him for an hour or two of recreation."

"We would be very grateful, Messire. We have the wherewithal to divert him all night..."

"Divert him by day. The night doesn't worry him."

"He likes to sleep?"

"Yes, yes. Occupy yourself with the day."

"Well, by day we'll divert him so well that he won't think about eating or drinking."

"That would be inconvenient. I like eating and drinking. If Monseigneur doesn't eat or drink, I can do no more nor less than him."

"Our minstrels can sing him the most pleasant romances there are: Parthenopex, the Round Table, the Holy Grail, Renaud de Montauban..."

"Hmm! I prefer other things to your romances. They're full of long amours, and Monseigneur likes them short—and then, the style is old."

"Say what you prefer: lays, fables, ballads..."

"Hmm! Hmm!"

"Songs? Oh, that will please Monseigneur d'Orléans, who is such a good poet himself, and to accompany us we have the bagpipe, harp, buccinas, psalterion, rebec, sackbut, theorbo, mandora..."

"Amen, amen! Recreate us well and you'll see deniers flow into your purse."

"The first to fall won't make a loud noise."

"It's dry? All the more reason to amuse us; but don't you know anything else but songs?"

"Oh, yes. Add that, personally, I'm not awkward with goblet tricks, for, in addition to my talent as a player of Mysteries, I know several métiers...and even more."

"Ah! You have a talent for playing Mysteries? Well, we'll judge it; but the mysteries...I prefer are serious. Can't you finish cheerfully, as the Prince of Fools does, so it's said."

"You're talking about devilries and moralities? Our cart isn't rich in scenery...and that would be quite long."

"Can your brethren not represent something without scenery?"

"It's difficult. Ah! Wait! I remember that we have one that's easy to construct; it's one of the nine scaffolds that we set up to play the great mysteries. It's the Mouth of Hell."

"Damn! What a name!"

"It could be introduced here and set up between the two pillars at the back."

"Well, give the orders yourself."

At the point the varlet returned, having learned that the wounded men were not in any danger.

"That's good. In that case, varlet, accompany the Brother of the Passion; lower the drawbridge and bring his men here."

The seneschal had difficulty dissimulating his contentment. The Mouth of Hell would certainly recreate Monseigneur better than a hanging.

While the varlet and the minstrel were outside, the seneschal resumed his pose in the armchair, and was soon snoring.

After ten minutes, not hearing any more noise, Mariette opened the door of her hiding place and, believing herself to be alone, advanced into the hall; but as she was about to reach the door hidden by the portrait, the sonorous snore of the seneschal caused her to shiver, and immediately, she heard a great rumor in the distance that was drawing nearer. She returned very quickly to her refuge, like a frightened mouse, and closed the door, at the moment when the seneschal woke up to receive the Fraternity of the Passion.

On seeing the scenery that had been taken from the cart and brought in, the seneschal experienced a panic similar to the one that had seized Aubert Le Flamenc at the apparition of Satan. The scenery escaped analysis as to painting; as to structure, it represented a fantastic beast, of which the Tarasque of Provence can give some ideas. It was the maw of a horrible monster, a mythological dragon, a mixture of everything animality has of the most hideous, which the casual brush of a Medieval painter giving it life, though, respiration and color, had reproduced with so much strangeness, in accordance with the ideas of the century, that the seneschal looked around, to see whether one of the long painted claws might be reaching over his head in order to seize him by the hair—a lugubrious idea that dominated him throughout the time that the minstrel monk employed in directing the placement of the scenery.

An incontestable proof of civilization is the progressive march of scenic play in a people, and when one remembers the departure of that march on the chariot of Thespis, splashed with lees, to arrive by jolts from rut to rut as far as the great centuries of Greece and Rome, was it not permissible for the fool of Charles VI, the Prince of Fools, to boast of holding his place in the conduct of the chariot? Was Master Gonin not the Thespis of the fifteenth century? He was *en route* for the station that saw Corneille and Molière, but there were still several steps to go. However, from mysteries to farces, a great rut had been crossed.

The minstrel monk presided over the adaptation of the horrific décor; when it was finished, he approached the seneschal.

"Oh, Monsieur, we have experienced many disappointments since our tour of the provinces, and we have come back as poor, ill-clad and dry as hanged men in summer. Oh, what has become of the time when we represented the Mystery of the Passion in all its splendor? A Mystery of fourteen thousand lines and eighty-six tableaux, with three hundred and ten characters, imitating the deeds and voices of the saints of both sexes, the evangelists, the apostles, the judges, the executioners, the soldiers, the good and bad thieves and Pontius Pilate, who figured in the great mystery of the suffering, death and resurrection of Our Lord Jesus Christ! Oh, the decorations! Paradise, Purgatory, Limbo, Hell, Jerusalem, Golgotha and other places as remarkable. What beautiful workmanship there was! I played God the Father in a fine embroidered surplice with a tiara, stole and rochet steaming with gold and diamonds, surrounded by angels magnificently clad in God's livery, blazoned with his armories, which are cross and stars on a field of azure strewn with sand..."

"How beautiful that must have been!"

"Sublime, Messire. Oh, our profession was venerated then, equal to that of Churchmen! But it only lasted for a time. The bourgeois of the towns started to play mysteries themselves. And God knows how the scholars and the low clergy have mounted the boards since the invention of farces by that rogue Master Gonin. We remained without work; we bit our fingernails to the elbows. It was necessary to live, though; so, what became of our decorations and our magnificent costumes? I'm ashamed to admit it, but we ate Purgatory in Tours, the earth in Rochefort and Paradise in Bordeaux."

"Ate, without drinking?"

"No, to our misfortune. Only Hell remains to us. Look, the scenery that has just been set up."

"It is well-named. As soon as I saw it, I felt a chill."

"But its mission is not to freeze people."

"Ha ha! I can see that you're a cheerful companion."

"Yes a good devil. That decoration serves us in many plays, the taste of the century being for devilries."

"Devilries are moral works. They show the malevolence of the Spirit of Darkness, against whose temptation the Christian must be on guard."

"Well said, Messire. But the populace attaches attention more to sorcerers and witches with beards bleeding pigs, composing filthy afterbirths with ordures, philters for doing harm. The common people take pleasure in the spectacle of the procuresses of the Sabbat, whipping one another with the entrails of dogs, uttering hoarse cries and dancing astride broomsticks with the accompaniment of indecent words. They burst out laughing when they see Monseigneur Satanas, mounted on a winged dragon, projecting fire and smoke through his nostrils of a horse with horns. But they cease laughing when, in the midst of the mewling of cats in rut, legions of toads, reptiles and birds of prey of every species appear, in the midst of which virgins in white robes are frolicking innocently, representing souls pure of any corruption, followed by the Holy Father carrying a stoup in one hand and asperging the demon with the other, to make him flee, howling!"

At that last depiction, the seneschal, who was as fearful of the Devil as Aubert Le Flamenc, was seized by a new tremor.

Master Gonin, who knew what he was saying, did not appear to perceive that effect of terror, and made a lyrical escape into the distance, in order to finish astounding his man.

"What a difference there is," he cried, "between the present art and the ancient art! In order only to touch one point, what a distance there is between our witches and the Eumenides of Aeschylus! Their fatal heads with the black gaze, twisted eyebrows, thick lips, cured by divine disgust for the crimes of the earth, respiring the somber enthusiasm of justice and chastisement; while the witches of Christianity, revolting imitations of the ancient furies, only represent the instincts of sin, the temptations of the demon..."

"Ugly as they are," interrupted the seneschal, "they're true. Our religions orders belief in them, and I believe in them; otherwise, what would become of the evil of Hell? Friend, your language reeks of the pagan and heresy."

"Ha ha, Messire, so I've played my satanic role well, since you've taken it seriously? That's a foretaste of the devilry you're about to witness."

"Hah ha! That's a good joke. Truly, then, it was a kind of prologue that you were reciting to me? I'll laugh at it for a long time."

With that laughter, the seneschal got up, in order to approach the Mouth of Hell, entirely set up, in order to examine it at his leisure, while the minstrel monk, wiping his brow, moist with the warmth that he had put into his classical peroration, said to himself: *Sow pearls before swine like that, and you'll reap thrusts of the snout!*

Then, plunging himself in the thought of the mission for which he had taken the responsibility; he was thinking about the consequences of its possible failure when a hand was placed on his shoulder and a muffled voice said to him: "Prince of Fools!"

Oh, said Master Gonin to himself, shuddering. *Recognized and doomed, not to say hanged!*

He turned round and saw a hooded Brother of the Passion.

"Aubert," he said to him, semi-reassured. "I forbade you to leave the cart and penetrate here. Your impatience and jealousy might compromise everything; you promised me otherwise!"

For all response, the monk raised his hood, and the Prince of Fools was thunderstruck by the apparition. Instead of one jealous individual, were there two? This one was more terrible than the other.

Laving Master Gonin stupefied, the monk headed for the door of the cabinet where Mariette was hiding, opened it, and went in, without the seneschal, who was occupied in examining the Mouth of Hell, perceiving the new devil.

It needed nothing less than the arrival of Étienne Mustau, hastening to inform his cousin that the pulley and counterweight had be set up, by means of a traverse fitted to the tops of the capitals, in order to facilitate the play of the Mouth of Hell, for the Prince of Fools to emerge from the stupor into which the apparition of the monk had thrown him.

Mariette was no less surprised by the entrance of the companion who had come to share her retreat.

He came in menacing, but it appears that an explanation followed rapidly, which did not appease the monk, but deflected his anger.

Mariette could not respond to all his questions. She did not know the name or rank of the person who had filled the role of her protectress, and it was perhaps the name and rank that the monk expected. Mariette could not even explain the secret of the moving painting, for the words of hatred and vengeance that escaped the monk caused Madame de Cauny to fear that her protectress might be unable to use the mysterious door in her turn, to escape a great danger.

In the meantime, the Prince of Fools and his cousin Étienne had been to rejoin their friends behind the Mouth of Hell, and the varlet Humbert came to inform the seneschal that Monseigneur, informed of the agreeable surprise that was being prepared for him, would not be long delayed in coming to the banqueting hall, followed by all the personnel of the château.

"All the personnel?" asked the seneschal, very surprised.

"Yes, Messire, except for the wounded men who cannot move their arms and legs. Oh, Monseigneur is good; he wants everyone here to be amused.

"So, varlets, archers, men-at-arms?" the seneschal asked again."

"All of them, indistinctly. Monseigneur has even ordered the archers to leave their weapons in the guard-room, in order that the clinking doesn't trouble the scenic representation."

"Oh, the good prince, the good prince! Can one imagine that a vassal or a vassale would refuse to acquit such a just and natural right? No, it's inconceivable. If I ever marry, I shall be the first to claim that honor for Madame la Sénéchale. Oh, the good prince. No so, Humbert? And you too?"

The varlet made a semblance of not having heard, muttering between his teeth: "The seneschal is the wood of which bagpipes are made."

XIV. THE FARCE

Thanks to Satan, this day will fulfill my hopes.

In an apartment situated on the first floor of the fleuronned, blazoned castle decorated with arabesques and equipped with balconies, an apartment whose luxury was in keeping with the exterior ornamentation, a young man was lying on an Oriental bed, his elbow on a cushion, in a meditative attitude. He was gazing in a melancholy fashion at an admirable young woman asleep in an armchair a few paces away. That young woman was running the risk of a terrible vengeance, while the fortunate sensualist for whom she was taking the risk was only experiencing for her, at that moment, what any man, even Don Juan, feels before a truly beautiful creature whose body is a poem for the senses.

The thought of the dreamer wandered in the midst of the ruins of the manor of Cauny, the black mass of which could scarcely be distinguished on the distant summit, and the old tower of which was outlined against the clear blue of the sky like a gray cloud.

The beauty of the young man received an exceptional attraction from the warm and soft sadness spread over his physiognomy, ordinarily smiling. Implacably skeptical in amour, he found himself now under the charm of a dream, engendered by the memory of the vanished reality.

His beard and his hair had not received their usual accommodation. Usually so careful of his person, so attentive to the slightest disorder of his garments and the slightest negligence in his adornment, he had given no thought to his toilette.

His high forehead, his large eyes, between blue and gray-green, of a charming softness and an expression almost unknown to the proud children of the Occident, had an omnipotent attraction for the women that he betrayed remorselessly, without ingratitude, convinced that amour is only a game of chance, the patrimony of the most skillful and the most inconstant. He had had many mistresses, and had never been in love.

His supple and perfectly formed figure announced grace, strength and ardor. But at that moment, the grace was languid and the strength vanquished; the ardor alone twisted him silently in a dream, at the poignant thought of knowing that his dear Mariette was in the power of a rude soldier to whom he had only ceded her in order to take her back more easily.

For the first time, Louis d'Orléans was jealous—so he was in love, or was close to loving.

Undoubtedly, it is necessary not to compare the love in question with that of Abelard for Héloïse, although the savant was far inferior to the savante; but between the unsatisfied Isabeau de Bavière and the overly sentimental Marguerite de Hainaut, the repentant Mariette d'Anghuien retained or had recovered the savor of a chastity still to be seduced, and the prince desired her as if he had not possessed her.

Orléans, whose abandonment of Mariette to Aubert Le Flamenc ought to have been simulated, in the sense that the honor of the former would be saved and the child whose mother she would be would have a father, was far from thinking that he would be separated from her for long, for more than a day. After having had her abducted by his seneschal, he had counted on keeping her for himself alone, knowing the measures he could take in order to distance the ex-captain of his arbalestiers, if necessary, from the conjugal roof.

But the armed resistance of Aubert, confounding a company of archers, five of whom were dangerously wounded, corroborated by Mariette's flight, had thwarted his plans.

Marguerite had revealed everything to him, or believed she had told him everything, not without violent reproaches. To the reproaches of an amorous woman he had responded with caresses, and sentimental women are credulous. Marguerite had calmed down under kisses, gone to sleep under arguments, and Louis was lying back, melancholy, when a flash of light suddenly traversed his mind.

Was not the seneschal preparing a surprise for him?

Had he not been promised music?

The frivolous man awoke from his reverie and woke Marguerite from her slumber. He found her beautiful and relegated the image of Madame de Cauny once again to a covert of his heart. The duchesse covered herself with a long veil, and the two lovers soon entered the banqueting hall, changed into a theater.

The audience, composed of twelve of fifteen people, acclaimed the couple, and the music commenced.

It was not too discordant for music of the fifteenth century. It was the prelude, and the Mouth of Hell opened to give passage to a bizarrely costumed child.

"It's the prologue," said the seneschal.

"He has a beautiful appearance," said the duc.

The audience uttered an expressive "Oh!" of admiration.

The door of the cabinet opened slightly. The heads of Mariette and the monk, who could not be seen, since the spectators had their backs to them, appeared momentarily.

"Do you know who that woman is?" asked the monk's gaze.

"No," said Mariette, with a movement of the head.

Madame de Cauny returned rapidly to her hiding-place. The monk remained, and the prologue continued.

THE PROLOGUE OF THE JUGGLER IN HELL

Salut! You will hear marvels
If with all your ears
You savor my words.
Soon, in the hall
Lucifer will appear
In the moral farce
Of the juggler in hell.
You will see the angel
Who, come from above,
By a strange device
Will make him ashamed;
The juggler for sure
Into the demon's abode
Will enter, it's said,
Doors open,
For he was
When on earth
He lived,
A lover
A debauchee
A drunkard
A beater
A piper
A robber

A handler
A captain
Of crooks;
Perhaps, in sum,
Cut-throats
Very nearly
A very honest man.
"Come," says Satanas
"That I might embrace you
I have for you, my lad
A good place.
Maintain the fire for me
Beneath my great cauldron,
For I'm going to earth
To take a stroll.
If one of the souls
Is lost, mark my words.
I'll hang you by the throat.
Here begins the action:

The mouth of hell opened to let the child reenter. There was loud applause

"Good God!" said the duc. "I know this one; it's a fine story. To whom are these fine lines owed?"

"I think to the poet Cretin, the author of the royal songs."[33]

"This Cretin is a great poet."

The Mouth of Hell yawned again, very broadly this time, and allowed the empire of Satan to be glimpsed in its interior, with the cauldron of the damned in the center.

---

[33] This confirms that the reference is to the sixteenth-century Guillaume Cretin, famous for his "royal songs" of 1527.

The juggler was maintaining the fire under the cauldron, above which heads were seen appearing and disappearing in the vapors of the boiling water.

The assembly shivered, thinking that such torture awaited every sinner that the Church had not absolved, when the soul was separated from the body.

Then the following dialogue was established:

A SOUL: I'm burning, burning!

THE JUGGLER: You're only here for that.

(*He plunges him back in with a thrust of the spade. An angel descends from the sky.*)

THE JUGGLER: What does he want?

THE ANGEL: Bonjour, Master.
I ought to recognize you;
Up there you were a good player
Of dice.

THE JUGGLER: You do me honor.

THE ANGEL: Hell's band has gone
Let's play a game.

(*He shows him a table and dice.*)

THE JUGGLER: Messire, I have no money.

THE ANGEL: Good, I have enough for both of us.

THE JUGGLER: How can I put up a stake?

Truly, I only have my shirt.

THE ANGEL: Put five or six souls in play;
So few will not be missed.

THE JUGGLER: No, Monseigneur, that bat
Will eat me when he returns,
Alive, or rather quite dead!

THE ANGEL: Look at these gold coins shining...

THE JUGGLER: Are they very good?

THE ANGEL Listen, how they ring!

(*He taps them against the cauldron.*)

THE JUGGLER: Oh, how those coins shine!
That dazzles me...

THE ANGEL: For two souls...

THE JUGGLER: One, no more.

THE ANGEL (*giving him the dice*): Throw.

THE JUGGLER Put the money on the table.

(*He throws the dice.*)

THE ANGEL: Chance will favor you;
Three, five and two, that makes ten.

THE JUGGLER: And you fourteen...accursed dice!

Two souls!

(*The game continues*.)

THE ANGEL: Six, four and three, thirteen
Me: double six and four, sixteen

THE JUGGLER: Damn! Ten souls at once!

THE ANGEL: That's a lot, Master

THE JUGGLER: Ace, four and three!

THE ANGEL (*before throwing the dice*):
What sort of people, friend,
Do you have in your cauldron?

THE JUGGLER: Many respectable people;
I don't say faultless,
But all fine fat monks,
Seigneurs, merchants, judges, canons
But…throw, then!

THE ANGEL: Six, five and two.
Three times as much as you; I'm lucky!
That makes thirteen souls in all.

THE JUGGLER: By all the saints there are in Rome
I've been very unlucky today.

THE ANGEL: All it takes to win all that back
Is one good throw.

THE JUGGLER: Yes, I'll bet fifty.

It's the Devil that's tempting me
It's not for his profit, thought!
By the poor man that I am,
I'll win! I've double four
And six.

THE ANGEL: Are you going to beat me, then?
Double six and five.

THE JUGGLER: That's too much.
I'll double.

THE ANGEL: You lost again!
Truly my luck is strange!

THE JUGGLER (*furious*): You're a cheat, my angel!
For an inhabitant of the holy place
That isn't good.

THE ANGEL: Whoever loses gambling
Always say he's been cheated.

THE JUGGLER: Indeed!
But don't touch (that's another story)
The cauldron...

(*He points at the cauldron.*)

THE ANGEL: Why not?

(*He touches the cauldron.*)

THE JUGGLER: I'll fall upon you, rogue,
Cheat, and pluck your wings!

So saying, he throws himself upon the angel, who, flying away, tips the cauldron over with a flick of his wing. Immediately, a multitude of people of every rank and costume emerge, who flee out of the Mouth of Hell and spread out among the audience, laughing heartily at the good trick played on the juggler.

The seneschal laughs more loudly than the others and cries: "Oh! The souls are fleeing!"

The duc repeats several times: "A fine morality!"

Everyone says his word about the devilry.

Finally, silence is reestablished; the juggler resumes his role:

THE JUGGLER: Well, my affairs are fine!
By Death, what will Satan say
When he returns? Ah! I hear him

(*He leaps into the hall. Enter Satan.*)

SATAN: I can't do any more… I'm swimming…
What does all this mess signify?

Here, the bursts of laughter redoubled, so nicely did the well-made-up actor mime amazement.

Louis d'Orléans, forgetting his mistress, pride and dignity, held his sides and called to the Prince of Fools, unrecognizable by virtue of his prodigious art of disguise and changing his voice: "Oho, Master Satan you're well caught! All your cuisine has gone to the Devil. Ha ha! Gone to the Devil! It's rather to God that it's necessary to say! Ha ha!"

"Ho ho!" said the seneschal, clutching his belly in both hands, as if he were preventing a balloon from deflating.

"Hee hee hee!" said the archers and the servants; and Master Gonin could see his audience oscillating and swaying under the breath of his farce.

The gaiety was redoubled when Master Satan, very angry, addressed the public:

"What have you to laugh at down there, then, stirring like a swarm of flies in a ray of sunlight? By my head and my horns, am I so funny? Well, I only have one more thing to say, which is that I'm Satan for real! And I want my souls back. To me! Head and blood!"

At the Satanic oath, the frightened souls drew nearer to the spectators, crying: "Mercy!"

The members of the audience, entering into the role of protector, still laughing, held out their arms to the poor souls, who attached themselves tremulously to their respective neighbors as ivy attaches itself to an elm.

Satan appeared to be taking his role seriously, and tragically. He clamored, in a Stentorian voice that seemed superhuman: "I have you in my power, do you hear? It's my turn to laugh. I'll make a legion of devils surge forth from underground, which will carry you away."

A glacial shiver ram through the assembly. Quavering exclamations were heard from all points:

"What did he say?"

"It's in the play!"

"No,"

"Yes."

"I have no vein within me that isn't throbbing!"

The fat seneschal cried: "The clown is drunk."

Riblet and Humbert vociferated: "You seem to us, fine talker, to have a forked tongue!"

Under the pretext of reassuring the duchesse, Louis d'Orléans clasped her in his arms and said, laughing: "It's a farce, my friends, a simple farce that will be explained to you."

Satan continued, redoubling his thunder:

"Go, go, my companions, go! Seize, bind and take the souls, and strike, if any resist!"

At the first cry of "Go, go!" the protective arms extended to the poor souls found themselves instantly seized and bound. The demons threatened the most recalcitrant with weapon hidden beneath their costumes.

Into that trap the monk from the cabinet launched himself upon the Duchesse de Nevers, lifted her veil, recognized her, uttered a sonorous cry, quite distinct from the tumult of those cries, showed his fist to the ceiling, holding it with the gesture in order to invoke the heavens directly, and returned to the cabinet.

That coup by the men of the farce was made as if it had been rehearsed for a long time; in the blink of an eye, no defender of the château was in a state to defend himself.

Master Gonin's men, as he had boasted, had been recruited among rogues of every kind: thieves, beggars, malingerers, gluttons, frauds, sharpers, wretches, pariahs and ruffians—in sum, in every category of Bohemia, exercised at an early age is trickery and, on occasion, knife-work. Gonin had found there intelligences cast out by the feudal system. He had made them capable actors for the epoch, actors who were more strolling players, true jugglers who combined bodily flexibility with the arts of covering oneself with artificial wounds, of counterfeiting, and, above all, of cutting purses.

Gonin had said to them: "Down with routine and the beggar's wallet! Jerusalem, which gave us the son of God, lied in sending us today the Brothers of the Passion to represent the mysteries under the porches of cathedrals. Let's mingle with that holy troupe, while reserving ourselves a pagan temple, alongside the Christian one."

There and then, the Carefree Children were created. As to the troubadours, the tellers of legends, the singers of ballads, the Northern bards and the Southern bards, châteaux, palaces and towns had opened their doors to the Carefree Children. It seemed impossible and sacrilegious not to listen to their moralities

That is why the trap was so easy to set at the Château de Beauté.

XV. THE ORGY

Let's drink, drink, drink
Like five hundred pigs!

The Prince of Fools, as we have seen, was a great artiste and a great conspirator. Machiavelli, who wrote comedies, would have applauded him.

He leapt from his stage into the hall and went straight to the Duc d'Orléans, at the moment when the latter, although tightly tied up, had found a means to draw his dagger from its sheath and was threatening Mustau, the juggler, who was guarding him. The Prince of Fools snatched it from his hands.

"Hey, my good seigneur, give me that jewel, which is only good for picking teeth, in truth. Now, go without making a noise to surprise the guards in their towers. As for you, prisoners of Hell, silence! Let no one budge, or cry out, or breathe a word, or I swear that the first one who whimpers will be garroted round the neck, as one ties a sack.

Then, spotting Aubert Le Flamenc he said: "Hey, friend; everything went like wax; here's your wife." He indicated Marguerite, still veiled. "Hmm," he said, you'll admit, friend that I'm a good devil; I could have snapped her up in my turn."

"Oh, Monseigneur," said Aubert, in a submissive and suppliant tone of reproach. "You have so many others, and that would have been unworthy of you."

"Aubert, here!" marveled the Duc d'Orléans."

"Aubert, said Gonin, relaxing in his majesty, "You asked for our omnipotent aid to reclaim your wife,

142

treacherously stolen by Louis d'Orléans; here she is, take her!"

"My dear Mariette, how you must have suffered!" said Aubert to Marguerite.

The duchesse recoiled in fear toward Orléans; the latter had neither the time nor the sang-froid to advise her to profit from the error and flee.

"Back!" he cried.

Aubert, transported by anger, drew his dagger and was about the strike the prince when Gonin interposed himself. "Friend, it's necessary not to take women by force."

Poor Aubert, subjugated by the Devil, lowered his head.

At the same time Mariette, opening the door of the cabinet, advanced and said in a simple tone: "Here I am, Messire; I'm ready to go with you wherever you judge it appropriate to conduct your wife before God and before men.

That had the effect of a truly theatrical scene on everyone. Even Gonin could not understand it; nevertheless, he did not allow his profound surprise to appear, and continued with an admirable presence of mind in his role as suzerain.

"Aubert Le Flamenc," he said, majestically, "you know our convention. Juggler, have him given two horses and two of our men to accompany him for ten leagues. They can rejoin us afterwards at the place they know."

"But can I not be arrested, having no royal pass, required to travel in the provinces?" Aubert replied, having only one care in his delight.

"That's true—and here's one," riposted Gonin, handing him a folded slip of paper that he had taken from his pocket. "Nothing's lacking—here's the king's seal."

Aubert added in a low voice: "And the name of Carpalin, which I must bear in future! Decidedly, I have a good fighter; he really is Satan in person."

"What are you muttering internally? Ah! something's lacking? Money? Here's some, and when you want more, address yourself to me. I'll always have some at your service, in my pocket…or in the pocket of the first passer-by, which is the same thing. *En route*, now!"

Mariette handed him a folded piece of paper that the monk had given her in the cabinet. Gonin took it and said: "What's this?" Then, having read the inscription, he added: "Ah! Yes, it's for you, Aubert, or rather for another, to whom you're charged with delivering it when you pass through Paris."

Aubert took the missive in one hand, drew Mariette away with the other, and left, followed by two Carefree Children.

The Prince of Fools continued his role as a great administer of justice: "I'm resuming my functions, Louis d'Orléans."

At his name, the duc raised his head. Since Mariette's appearance he had fallen into a strange absorption. *She was there*, he said to himself.

"Louis d'Orléans," Gonin continued, "your life has been, thus far, full of disorders and mad expenditure. In order to satisfy your hectic passions, you have pressurized the poor and insulted their poverty with your luxury. You are going to be subject to the chastisement you merit. I am going to take possession of all the riches contained in this château, which originate from seizures operated around you by your seneschals, beginning with that fat wheezer there—silence, Seneschal!—your searchers and riders—shut up, Riblet. Those riches will return to the people, from whom they came. I'll take charge of the division. Now, if you have some reply to make, you may speak."

"I have to reply," said the prince, "that you are nothing but a miserable bandit. I'll have you boiled in the Place de Grève as soon as I can."

"Well said, Monseigneur."

"You'll be burned as a fraud and forger, devil as you say you are."

"Am I not?"

"A sorcerer, perhaps—but Satan? No. If you're the Devil, swear by God that you are. That will prove you even better than your rascality. Look at this venerable relic of Saint Denys. There is no magic or spell that does not dissipate before it, and if you were anything other than a highway robber and vagabond, it would already have made you go back underground."

Gonin shrugged his shoulders in pity, saying: "Poor man! Credulous by virtue of credulity! Well, you'll confess, at least, that I'm a sorcerer of the foremost strength."

Immediately ridding himself of his Satanic accoutrements, including his horns and face of a goat, he appeared as a heavily-built and muscular knight, armored in iron, with a helmet on his head, regulation knee-guards, arm-bands and thigh-guards. Then, kneeling like a gallant paladin before the duchesse, whom he had divined, he said: "Don't be afraid, Madame. You will remain a spectator of this mystery until the end. It is, in any case, reaching its conclusion."

He got up and addressed himself again to the Duc d'Orléans.

"It's true, Monseigneur, that I'm not Satan in person, nor even his delegate. I'm only pursuing my role, nothing more. But agree that the devilry I've played is moral enough for you to remember it—so applaud!"

"Truly, you're a master clown…although it goes a bit far…but have the woman who has departed brought back, and you can take from here anything you wish."

"Not so loud!" said Gonin, casting a glance at the cabinet.

At the same time, the Duc d'Orléans darted one at the duchesse whom he was denying, and added: "I can only applaud that denouement."

"That cannot be, Monseigneur. The beauty is already far away, and I'm not ready to set you free."

"Scoundrel!"

"Oh, that's a strange fashion of negotiating. Am I not the master here? Can I not hang you all, if it pleases me…which would, in fact, be safest for me. For, let's reason... It's admitted…but here come some of my men laden with booty. Is that all you've found?"

"Yes, Master."

"Search again…true God! What beautiful cups. Put them on the banquet table. Someone bring wine, the best. Bring up from the cellars as much as you can carry. These Messieurs are going to reason with us, aren't you, Monseigneur?"

"What! How can we?" said Orléans, mockingly. "Are we not tied up?"

"Pardon me, but bracelets don't hinder the articulation of the phalanges. The fingers can seize a cup. We'll inform you of the game. Let's resume. Admittedly, as I was saying, "I'm a brigand, a bandit, a thief, a sorcerer—anything you wish. I'm myself and no other. Your epithets strike the air with a sound, that's all. It's also

146

evident, and this is positive, that I'm the master of the château, and that I have enough men to sustain a siege, if necessary."

"True God!" said the seneschal, agitated on his stool as if to break it. "Are there three hundred of you?"

"Three hundred and some," replied Gonin, indifferently. "Juggler, are they all at their posts?"

"The ramparts are garnished."

"That's good. Has care been taken to set up a gibbet for the recalcitrant, if there are any?"

"Look out of the window, Master."

In fact, a gallows rose up in the garden, and the rope was swinging in the wind. That sight produced a salutary effect and good order among the vanquished.

"I believe," the Prince of Fools continued, "that the most certain means of our withdrawing in safety with our booty is to kill you all before leaving..."

A general cry interrupted the speaker, who did not seem at all moved but it.

"That's my thinking—I can't be mistaken. If you have some better counsel to give me, in your interest and ours, speak."

"Listen," said the prince, "since the circumstances are such that a prince of the blood is obliged to yield before a man like you, I'll give you my word as a prince not to pursue you in any way and to let you go with the fruit of your expedition."

"Find me something else, and let's hurry."

"By Saint Louis! I'm very good to have made you such a proposition."

And I'm asking you for your advice. Aha! Here's the wine. Listen; I've had an idea that will cut through all difficulty. I'll enable you to die decently and agreeably."

A rumor of lamentation went up.

Humbert, having struck the banqueting table with his irons, as if to break it, was immediately seized and dragged out of the hall. Soon, his cadaver was seen swinging from the long arm of the gibbet

That tragic and rapid incident paralyzed all complaint.

"I'll only enable you to die for a few hours," Gonin continued, "After which you'll resuscitate, fresh and hearty. I give you my word. That's agreeable to you, I hope."

"Hang us immediately, then, like poor Humbert," said the prince, "since you can and since you dare. But cease playing with us."

"Oh, you agree that I can, if I dare. Well, I can do more." Then, extending his arms toward the hanged man, he shouted: "Dead man, unhang yourself, walk, and come here."

At that injunction the cord broke, the cadaver fell, got up, walk, and came to resume its place in the hall— but it was as livid as a man who was returning from the other world, and no longer had any desire to rebel.

"All this astonishes you, Prince? I see that it has given you the gloss to my allegory. Here's the wine. You're going to drink until you fall to the floor, dead drunk, only to wake up twenty-four hours later. In the meantime we'll be on our way. Do you understand? The means are very amusing and entirely new, a double condition to which I hold hard, exercising my estate as an artiste, wanting glory as much as profit.

The duc smiled. "It's necessary to have a good heart against fortune. I'll console myself for having been pillaged by such a wily clown. Let's drink, then, since it's necessary. Let's drink until drunkenness and slumber.

Your means aren't new, this won't be the first time that wine has enabled me to forget the contrarieties of life."

"Ah! That's well said. Untie Monseigneur and sit the prisoners down at the banqueting table, comfortably. One of you stand behind the seat of each of them, pitcher in hand, in the fashion of a cup-bearer, in order to pour the nectar constantly, and let none of you, Messieurs the archers, seek to deceive us by letting yourself fall under the table before being completely drunk; we know that condition too well! And then, to be more sure, we'll lock the doors. Juggler, I recommend the seneschal to you; take care of his great paunch until he capsizes...

"As for the two of us, Monseigneur...here's a little table of antique form, favorable to the sacrifice of our reason, which the god Fatum demands for the voice of his ministry. Drink from this broad-brimmed cup, as large as that of Cneius Somitius, the ancestor of Nero, who killed a freedman, having committed the fault of taking him back twice.

Emptying his cup in a single draught, the duc replied: "Oh! You're an erudite man!"

During the time in which the erudite man went to the juggler to fill an enormous amphora, Orléans whispered in Marguerite's ear: "Duchesse, you have the golden key. Take advantage of it in order to escape, and send me help."

"I'm thinking about it," she replied. "At the first opportunity, I'll take advantage of it."

While that exchange was taking place, the Prince of Fools, for his part, observed to his cousin Mustau that all was going well, and that once out of the château one of them would go to the right and the other to the left, in order to meet up in Paris where Madame la Reine, satisfied by a ruse of war that Messire Miltiades would not

149

have disavowed, would put him in possession of the charge of king of ribauds.

"And then, once there, try to be honest and you'll make your way…relatively honest. You'll be in the law and we'll still be in the craft. They're two professions that go hand in hand, one carrying the other. When you see yourself obliged to send one of ours to the gibbet— for in spite of my vigilance, there's always some carefree child who remembers his estate of thief, you'll employ the means that I taught you. In any case, our trial with Humbert succeeded perfectly."

"In fact cousin, it requires an apprenticeship. Humbert had a narrow escape; it was just in time that the noose stopped tightening."

"That would have been unfortunate. You wouldn't have done it deliberately; but it was impossible."

With that, after slipping into Étienne's hand the soporific powder to mix with the wine, Gonin returned to the duc, who drained his cup. As, in sum, that prince did not need to drink much to put him in a good humor, he almost was. That daze was sufficient for the present moment to bear away on its wing the whim of the previous one. With a word, Gonin had pushed him into antiquity, and he already saw Euterpe frolicking around him, with her symbolic attributes.

XVI. THE BLACK MONK

What voice us making itself heard?
Will another amour enchain you?
Be careful, for my tender heart
Will avenge itself on both.

There was a secret and powerful affinity between the poet prince and the literate clown.

Gonin, holding a cup in each hand and holding out the one that had received a pinch of powder, exclaimed: "Monseigneur, let's drink to the maids of honor of Madame Venus! To the three Graces: to the brilliant Aglaia; to Thalia, who inspires joy; and to Euphrosine, who rejoices the soul!"

The two glasses clinked, and there was a general clinking; the archers, varlets and bandits clinked joyfully. The wine was exquisite, old and from Beaune, the color of ox-horn, then supreme.

"In truth," said Orléans to Gonin, "I'm astonished by the métier you follow, literate as you appear to be...."

"Alas," replied the Prince of Fools, "that's exactly what doomed me. I had the misfortune to have a father who loved me very much, a poor workman who retrenched his subsistence as much as he could in order to put me out of his track. As my intelligence was awakened, he made me a cleric. I learned all the sciences: theology, chemistry and astrology, not to say magic. I forgot philosophy—oh, I was in full strength there. No one argued better than me on the metaphysics of Aristotle; but no one, also, broke more pewter trays and stoneware pot in the taverns. By night, it was something else.

With worthy companions I had learned to confound the two syllables *thine* and *mine*. I raided the smocks of belated bourgeois or laid siege to some money-changer on the great parvis. It was necessary to make up for the insufficiency of the paternal subsidy. When the revolt of the Maillotins broke out, I did not fail to take part in it, not only in deed but in words. I celebrated their prowess in verse..."

"Ah! You also caress..."

"The Muse? I crumple her, Monseigneur, like a true peasant... but we're forgetting our libations…come here, Juggler, and refill out cups."

Étienne Mustau rendered to his cousin's appeal, and the duc, having emptied his cup and allowed something to escaped that resembled a vulgar belch, cried joyously: Since you appear to me to be expert in the matter, it's necessary that I make you judge of a piece of verse of my fabrication..."

"I'm listening, Monseigneur."

"It's a song, a simple song dedicated to Madame Venus:

Begs presently.
 Humbly
Louis, Duc d'Orléans,
Who has long been
One of your obedient,
And between true lovers,
 Your servants,
In the times of youth
 Very pleasant,
Served you loyally.

And also, such is fate,
  Made the mistake
Of sending out of reach
The sole lady and mistress
To whom he made the promise,
In despair of comfort
  And distress,
That no princess ever had
  Or goddess,
For his heart is in accord.

"If the rest is similar, Monseigneur, spare me!"

"What, peasant! You dare to scorn a work by me, whom everyone declares to be the prince of French poets?"

"Prince, so be it," Gonin interrupted, pulling a significant face, "but poet, that's different, the same note as Charles d'Anjou, Thibaut de Champagne and Henry de Soissons."

"It doesn't have the gift of pleasing you, clown?"

"I prefer, I confess, Rutebeuf, Huon, Haisiaux and Courtebarbe."[34]

"Those are fine poets, as hard as their names, who have never read the troubadours, nor other Greek and Latin authors."

"That's true but they drank well, and found their inspiration in the wine bottle. You're sparing yourself...come on. Juggler, your song, to cheer up Monseigneur!"

"Here goes, Master!"

---

[34] The names are those of legendary troubadours.

Étienne Mustau intoned three verses, the chorus of which was sung by the Carefree Children:[35]

Cunning swains
And heavy goads
Are suzerains,
Of the high roads.

Crick, crock, clickety clink
Cheat, cheat...let's all drink!

From gibbet's rise
At the final dose
To Paradise
One is quite close.

Crick, crock, clickety clink
Cheat, cheat...let's all drink!

In that great port
One lives nicely
Without effort
And yet spicily.

Crick, crock, clickety clink
Cheat, cheat...let's all drink!

---

[35] The words of this song are difficult to translate literally, many belonging to an obsolete *argot* and others being non-sense syllables, and Gonin paraphrases its meaning in the text, so I have been content to attempt an improvisation that preserves the spirit of the original, and to duplicate the rhyme-scheme.

The prince's men had barely repeated the third refrain when they collapsed on the table and fell asleep.

The prince struggled again slumber and repeated once more:

Crick, crock, clickety clink

"I'll explain in vulgar language what the song means," said Gonin. "Thieves are the lords of the highways. Those who are hanged die closer to Heaven, and once with the good God they have good wine and white bread at their discretion. Can one find a sweeter moral?"

Orléans did not reply; he went to sleep in his turn, repeating:

Cheat, cheat...let's all drink!

"Goodnight, Monseigneur!" cried the Prince of Fools, gaily.

Having made sure that the archers and varlets were sound asleep, he hastened to get rid of his helmet, his armor and his coat of mail.

"It's time to pack the bags," he said to his men. "Let's go! But first, a word of warning: let those who don't want to be hanged hold their tongues."

The entire band, which had gathered, bowed and drank a stirrup cup, singing:

Let's drink as much, and break the pots.
As a hundred sols...oh, oh and oh!
To our hostess let's not pay our lots,
Apart from a credo and a ho and ho!

In a matter of minutes the Mouth of Hell was dismantled and transported to the cart, already laden with all the stolen booty.

That done, they set forth, around the wheel, because of the load and the potholes in the road, especially through the Bois de Vincennes.

As they were entering Paris through the gate of the Rue de Barbette a rider emerged launching his horse at full tilt along the road leading to the Bois de Vincennes. In the wood the horseman crossed the path of two monks mounted on placid mules; the monks moved to the side of the road, and when the rider had gone passed like lightning, one of the monks said to the other: "That man's running faster to misfortune than good fortune. He'll only reach his goal to slip in the blood.

He knew that full well, the mysterious monk, whose vengeance had prepared the catastrophe, who had lifted the veil of the duchesse and returned Mariette to Aubert Le Flamenc.

His companion made no reply; he was not in such a tragic humor; the Mouth of Hell in painted cloth sufficed for him.

Having reached the first courtyard of the Hôtel Saint-Pol, the two monks went into it, showing a royal pass. There, getting rid of their habits, one returned to the royal apartments and the other, passing under the arched door opening to the Rue de Tournelles, returned to his theater on the market square.

What had happened between those two individuals in the Château de Beauté before the departure of the Carefree Children? A brief but terrible scene.

The Duchesse de Nevers had pretended to be asleep in order to escape the vigilance of the demons who were masters of the château. When the latter had set forth under the conduct of Étienne Mustau, she opened her eyes, but she saw standing before her, contemplating her through the two holes of the penitent's mask, which hid the face entirely, the monk of the cabinet, in the company of a Brother of the Passion.

The monk had not gloved his hand, and the plump grace of the latter might have betrayed her, if the dagger with which she had suddenly armed herself and the words that emerged from her mouth, had not revealed an implacable rival.

Marguerite threw herself to her knees, pleading for her life; she would have implored in vain if the Brother of the Passion had not retained the raised arm and disarmed the monk who had come to punish with the authority of an accomplice.

The duchesse had fainted with fear and horror. When she came round, the furious monk and Master Gonin had disappeared; no one remained in the mute hall but the sleeping guests; the château was abandoned and open. She had not dared to quit Orléans, who was dreaming, when the sound of a galloping horse caused her to shudder, to stand up and look through the window to see what was happening outside, by the light of a splendid moon.

A rider, whom she recognized immediately, arrived at top speed. Quickly, she gave a kiss to her sleeping lover, and then ran to the door hidden by the painting. She opened it and disappeared into the subterranean labyrinth.

She was just in time. As that door closed, the one to the hall opened and Jean de Nevers irrupted into it.

A rapid glance found nothing suspect. With a resin torch he went to each guest and looked at him. When he reached Lois d'Orléans he was tempted to crush the torch on his face.

He contented himself with saying scornfully: "That's the man who intends to govern the realm! Poor country!" He added, with a deep sigh of menace: "I've been deceived. Woe betide the man who calumniated Marguerite!"

He mounted his horse again and went at a less rapid pace to the retreat of Saint-Saturnin, where he found his wife at prayer, gave her a conjugal accolade, recommended her to God, and returned to Paris to supervise the organization of the army corps that he was about to lead to Hungary.

On the way, however, he thought about the Château de Beauté, open to all comers, and the disorder that reigned there, of which he had no explanation, and he sent one of his officers, Raoulet d'Actonville,[36] at the head of a company of lancers to protect a princely residence that he called a den of abomination.

---

[36] This name appears in several chronicles as that of the man paid by Jean *Sans Peur* to kill the Duc d'Orléans; Jules Michelet reproduces it in his mammoth history of France, but the allegation is probably based of slanderous hearsay.

XVII. AUBERT LE FLAMENC

No, all is said, the livid and somber night
Like an inferno is about to light up.
The deceived man will work in the shadows,
His avenging arm will spread fear and tears.

In those days, fractioned France counted innumerable masters who, under the titles of prince, duc, comte and baron, although vassals of the crown, were more powerful than the man to whom they rendered homage.

One of the most important of those little States was the Duchy of Aquitaine, which the King of England had possessed since the marriage of Henry II with Aliénor de Guyenne, repudiated by the austere Louis le Jeune.

It was to Aquitaine that, on the order of Isabeau de Bavière, the Sire de Cauny and his wife went, at the gallop of two vigorous chargers. It was not without dangers that they traveled the distance separating the Château de Beauté from the small town of Coutras, where they counted on stopping. Hostelries were sparse and the roads unsafe.

They were installed there under the name of Carpalin, which the royal pass bore, and at first they lived an easy life there, thanks to the purse richly garnished with gold crowns that Gonin had detached with the thrust of a sickle from Monseigneur d'Orléans' belt—or rather, which he had seized royally, in order to give it to the deceived husband as a object of initial reparation, as compensation.

After a few months, the purse was exhausted, and the resources promised by the Prince of Fools did not arrive. Isabeau was rid of Mariette; she did not want to hear any further mention of her.

From his former position as clerk in his father's practice, Aubert had conserved a fine pen. He became a copyist of manuscripts and obtained work in the convents of Guyenne and Gascogne.

Aubert Carpalin toiled with all the more courage because he then believed himself to be the author of the fruit whose ripening he counted every day.

He made a new skin while laboring with the monks; his education was augmented; he obtained eloquence; everything brought him joy; but the softening of his forms did not extinguish within him the ferocity of the soldier.

He believed a little more in God and a little less in the Devil, but he believed furiously in his right to be the father of his children, and when there came to him, after six months of marriage, a son as fully-made and mature as a child of nine months, he nearly exploded with rage, and his wrath burst forth: "He shall die!"

"Mercy!" sobbed Mariette. "He isn't guilty!"

"He shall die, and you, and the traitor...."

"In the name of your mother, Messire..."

"My mother was an honest woman."

"I swear that I am a wife without reproach, although I have been a wilted maiden. The man who abused my youth has obtained nothing from Madame de Cauny. If I had consented to deceive you, they would not have snatched me from the Manoir de Cauny to transport me to the Château de Beauté. That poor child would have been born during a mission of a few months that the prince would have given you; appearances would have been saved. I didn't want to lend myself to that final infamy."

Aubert Le Flamenc reflected. Suddenly, he threw away the dagger with which he had armed himself, and said to Mariette: "You shall live."

"Mercy for my child."

"There's no need of mercy. Your life is useful to a project that has just illuminated my mind like an infernal flame, like an ardent ember brushed by a piece of ice."

From that day on, not a word was exchanged on that subject between the two spouses, strangers to one another henceforth, and Orléans' bastard grew in age, in strength and in health.

XVIII. THE MARKETPLACE

The donkey is made to populate the marketplace with
carrots,
Cabbages, pumpkins and bunches of salsify.
If the need to love is born in his soul,
Sentimentally, he brays his tender flame.
Let's go! Giddy up, wretch...

Jean de Nevers lost his father Philippe and became
Duc de Bourgogne some time after his return from the
Orient, where he had been subjected to harsh defeats and
had been taken prisoner by Bajazet, along with Boucicault.[37] He had returned from Hungary diminished, and
in order to recover his prestige he had flattered the people, mingled familiarly with the crowds, involving himself to the extent of shaking the hand of the executioner,
but he could not draw the masses into his hatred of
Orléans. The latter governed, in the name of the king,
with Isabeau, but slackly, like a man of pleasures, and
the people continued to be overloaded by the seigneurs
and the monks, a poor beaten donkey.

---

[37] The Ottoman Sultan nowadays known as Bayezid I defeated
the Christian forces at the battle of Nicopolis, but fell prey
himself to the Turco-Mongol warlord Timur—known as
Timur the Lame, or Tamerlane—in 1402. He is not the same
person as the eponymous character of Jean Racine's tragedy
Bajazet (1672). Jean *Sans Peur* won his nickname at the battle
of Nicopolis in 1396, but his recklessness there probably
harmed the Christian cause. He was ransomed after a year of
captivity.

During the captivity of Jean de Nevers, Orléans had gone to make war in Guyenne, but he had failed piteously under the walls of Blaye and had returned to Paris without laurels, but satisfied with his campaigns. He had discovered Mariette's retreat in Coutras and had her abducted again. He hid her in the Hôtel de Bohème, his vast dwelling, which was called by that name in memory of Jean de Luxembourg, King of Luxembourg, to whom it had belonged previously. That house was replaced by a palace built by Catherine de Médicis and subsequently became the Hôtel de Soissons and then the Cornmarket. Of its past, only a single column has been preserved, of the Doric order, the height of which surpassed eighty feet, and which Catherine went up in order to observe the constellations. Not far from there were the markets, established in 1278 by Philippe le Hardi along the wall of the cemetery of Les Innocents, for selling clothing, leather and shoes. Later the market was augmented with fish, vegetables and fruits, and all that attracted the populace; a pillory was established there, composed of an octagonal construction in masonry surmounted by a wooden lantern-tower. In the middle of that lantern-tower a mobile iron wheel was laced, pierced with holes, through which the heads and hands emerged of those condemned to be exposed to the gaze the public of housewives come to make their provisions, as well as donkeys laden with goods and braying competitively.

Close by, another spectacle attracted the curious: the theater in which the Prince of Fools had installed his errant troupe definitively.

Finally, under the pillars of the marketplace there was the shop of the father of Coline Demerre, whom we have seen in the court d'amour claiming the justice of that tribunal against the prolific prowess of the Duc d'Orléans.

Now, that barber was in the process of shaving the man-at-arms Riblet, our old acquaintance, who appeared to be about forty years old and was proud of his promotion in rank. He had just been telling a story, interrupted by the razor, and which he resumed when his beard was removed.

"Yes, friend Jehan," he said, "it was at the end of January in the year of Our Lord 1392; so, since we're in October 1407, it was more than fifteen years ago.[38] Two days before, the king's costume had caught fire in the masquerade in which he lost his reason completely, and, I repeat, we let ourselves be tied up like onions at the Château de Beauté."

"You were dealing with a very cunning fellow," said Demerre. "Who could it have been?"

"Perhaps the King of Argot, the great Coesre?"[39]

"Oh, no, that one, who has been known in these parts for thirty years and whose name is Jacques Pipelu, doesn't have his legs has himself drawn in a little carriage harnessed to two dogs when he sings his ballads."

"Then it was the Duc de Bohème! What does it matter? Anyway, to conclude the story, he left us all lying on the ground, like calves at the market of La Grève, no more capable of breathing a word than dead donkeys.

---

[38] As previously noted, the ball at which Charles VI was burned was in 1393, not 1392, and Jacob must have been born in that year, but the next few chapters must be set in the last months of 1407 in order to be consonant with known history, hence the adaptation.

[39] "Le grand coësre," king of the beggars, is featured in *Notre-Dame de Paris—1482*, so his presence here is anomalous.

Between us, that's because he gave us enchanted wine to drink. Perhaps we'd still be sleeping if a troop of the Duc de Nevers' arbalestiers hadn't come to shake us like plum trees. Monseigneur d'Orléans, whom the Duc de Bohème had served as cup-bearer in person, only woke up to dream aloud, and when the leader of the arbalestiers asked him what had happened to the rogues who had pillaged the château, he replied: 'The rogues are in your skin, rascal! Dare you still maintain that argot songs are worth more than my ballads, tensons, lays, virelays and sirventes?' He continued to spout nonsense of that sort, so that Jean de Nevers' men, unable to get anything out of him, began to beat the country at random to find the trail of the bandits, who were far away."

"And if you encountered the Duc de Bohème, as you call him, what would you do?"

"I wouldn't fail to have him arrested, and I hope they wouldn't fail to hang him. In the meantime, Master Jehan, here's an eagle denier for the week. But where's your boy? Hey, Jacob, come here, lad."

"Here I am. here I am, replied a young man of fifteen or sixteen, showing himself at the threshold.

"Do you know, Master Jehan, I saw him back in the time of your daughter, God rest her soul. She died very young, and her husband too. I didn't know him; he was a mason, wasn't he, and got crushed? You told me that."

"Yes, friend, crushed."

"He knew how to build children. The more he grows, the more he takes on a false appearance of Monseigneur d'Orléans."

"Yes, perhaps, but a false air, without the song."

"That's all right; it's better to resemble a prince than a pauper. It's a look, no doubt that your daughter would have received. She must have seen Monseigneur pass in great ceremony while she was pregnant. It takes no more to make the mistake; but it's the rule that women would rather look at a handsome, well-dressed seigneur glittering with gold than a bourgeois like you or a simple man-at-arms like me…and yet, for want of a prince, a man-at-arms in full dress, when appropriate…! You'll tell me that a bourgeois, when he's in service for the watch and has the means of bronze armor, like you, Master Jehan, can also catch a woman's eye, but it's still necessary for him to be well-built, otherwise he looks as if he's wearing kitchen utensils."

"Yes, friend, it's a look, nothing else."

"In favor of your resemblance to Monseigneur, here's a maille for you, child, but don't go gambling it…"

"Thank you, Master Riblet, but give it to a beggar," little Jacob replied, proudly, very satisfied to resemble a prince.

"Oho! You're as proud as the elder son of Samorabaquin![40] Enough chatter; I'm going back to the Hôtel de Bohème to prepare myself to accompany Monseigneur d'Orléans to the Augustins, where he has to go today, as well as Monseigneur de Bourgogne, to swear eternal reconciliation on the sacred host."

Riblet went away, muttering between his teeth: "He certainly has the look of Monseigneur d'Orléans. If he brought misfortune to the daughter, he brought good fortune to the father and the child!"

---

[40] Samorabaquin is a Turkish sultan mentioned in Froissart but otherwise obscure.

XIX. THE PILLORY

Oh, he whispered, here's deliverance.
Go, walk, be joyful, for your irons are broken
You have murmured vengeance long enough!
It will be accomplished on that perverse prince.

Three clients were waiting their turn after Riblet. They were well-to-do bourgeois who lived some distance away, and came twice a week, not only to have themselves shaved, but also to chat to one another: Master Guérin-Boisseau, the cobbler of the Pont-aux-Meuniers; Master Lescalopier, the hatmaker of the Rue des Tournelles; and Master Bournichon, the hosier of the Place Maubert.

The barber had called Jacob, who was his assistant. Jacob obeyed, pulling a face. He was irritated by having to stir himself for such vulgar practices. It was the face of Guérin-Boisseau that fell to the child; his father, before going to a meeting of the militia, was burnishing his armor, and he did not hurry, chatting with the bourgeois; the latter were in no hurry either.

"It is, I believe, the second time," said Master Bournichon, waiting his turn and sitting beside Master Lescalopier, who was also waiting, "Yes, the second time in two years, that the two ducs have been reconciled."[41]

---

[41] A reconciliation between Jean *Sans Peur* and the Duc d'Orléans was, in fact, attempted in 1407 in Paris, mediated by Isabeau, but in circumstances very different from those described here. Jean had marched on the city two years earlier

"It won't be the last," said Lescalopier, judiciously,

"Hmm! Hmm!" said the barber, ribbing his breast-plate.

Guérin-Boisseau took advantage of a respite that Jacob gave him, while passing his razor over his sleeve, to join the conversation. "This reconciliation doesn't presage anything good; the country will never be tranquil as long as the Duc d'Orléans is in power and he continues with the queen to pillage and dissipate the public fortune..."

Master Guérin interpreted himself with a cry. Jacob had nicked him.

"What's the matter" asked the barber.

"Your son has cut me."

"Why are you talking?" Jacob hastened to say, who could not tolerate anyone speaking ill of the Duc d'Orléans.

"Be careful, my son," observed the barber, gently.

"Grandfather, when the client opens and closes his mouth..."

"One gives warning before cutting."

"Bah! It's nothing," said Lescalopier

"This isn't, however," Guérin-Boisseau continued, "the shop of your colleague of the Cité, the surgeon who cut the throats of his clients to make mincemeat for the butcher next door, two years ago."[42]

---

with a force of a thousand knights, forcing Orléans and Isabeau to flee. Charles had a period of lucidity, as the story suggests, and did what he could to prevent open war, but the reconciliation never happened, Orléans being assassinated on his return to Paris.

[42] If this story really had been composed in 1830, this observation would predated by some fifteen years *The String of*

"Yes," the hatmaker replied, "but it was prosperous people to whom he addressed himself, not poor merchants ruined by the duties, taxes, seizures and credits of great seigneurs. Oh, Master Jehan, it's enough to make the stones in the ground weep, to see how unfortunate the poor people are this year, and it's the fault of those who govern us."

"Who are you talking to? I know one thing: out of ten clients, at least five are keeping their beards for the sake of economy.

And Jehan started rubbing his salad-bowl helmet more vigorously.

"All the evil comes from that Monseigneur d'Orléans," said Guérin-Boisseau, pushing away the razor in order to talk. Oh, if it were Monseigneur de Bourgogne, things would be different. What a worthy seigneur, not proud, to whom one can speak in the street as to a friend..."

"If you keep talking, I'll never finish shaving you," Jacob observed.

"You're right, child."

Resuming his posture in order to allow the office of the razor to continue, Master Guérin abandoned the reply to Lescalopier, who said: "Everyone knows the causes of

---

Pearls, the famous English penny dreadful that popularized the legend of Sweeney Todd, the "demon barber of Fleet Street," the plot of which is summarized here. On the other hand, a Parisian version of the urban legend in question, extracted from the memoirs of Joseph Fouché and referring to events in the aftermath of the 1789 Revolution, was published in 1825, and was therefore readily available in 1830—although not, of course, in 1407.

the king's malady. It's by enchantment and spells that the queen and the duc maintain his madness."

"Yes," said Jehan gravely, "And do you know what the queen's witchcraft is? I learned it from the Carefree Children I shave…"

"Well, what do they do?" asked his three interlocutors.

"They make images of the king in wax, which they prick with enchanted needles, and they also compose philters."

"Oh, those are just rumors that are going around," said Lescalopier.

"Only rumors? Yes, and there are also rumors that they're keeping our poor King Charles VI locked up in a low room in the Hôtel Saint-Pol, where he lives in squalid conditions, dressed in rags, and they often forget to bring him bread, while in the great halls, the queen and Orléans, surrounded by their favorites, are sitting at a table laden with exquisite dishes and generous wines! The people know all that, and one day they'll interrupt all those feasts and liberate the king!

The barber had hardly finished speaking when a great tumult broke out in the marketplace. Jehan Demerre went to the threshold to see what was happening in the street, and came back to say: "It's the King of Ribauds taking the condemned to the pillory."

The cobbler, whom Coline Demerre's son had finished shaving, and whose hair he was now combing, sighed and exclaimed: "Bankrupts, no doubt; they're taken every day. There are no longer any limits to that now, the bourgeois are so wretched. How can you expect a merchant to pay his debts when the great seigneurs don't pay him? Do you know how many creditors the Duc d'Orléans has? Eight hundred!"

"I know that as well as you do; I've furnished the curtains and hoods for his house for two years without seeing a maille."

"And he's had six hundred pair of socks from me."

"And six hundred pairs of half-pointed shoes from me for the men of his company. Every time he passes with his retinue on his way to see the queen, I say to myself: if everything that belongs to me were returned to my stock, those fine messieurs would be walking barefoot,"

"He gathered all his creditors together once," said Bournichon, "but only to have them beaten with sticks."

"That was to honor him," said Jacob, laughing, "since he has a knotty stick in his arms."

The Duc d'Orléans had indeed taken for an emblem a knotty staff, with the motto: "I wield it." The Duc de Bourgogne had chosen a scraper, with the motto: I hold it."

"Yes," retorted the barber, "but beware of the scraper!"

"The scraper won't scrape anything," said the young man, "And the stick will beat the dogs that bark."

"He talks like the son of a gentleman, the little clown," said Guérin-Boisseau. "And you put up with that, Jehan?"

"If you continue to warm my ears," said the barber, "I'll give you a good thrashing."

"You won't lift your hand to me twice!" replied Jacob, raising his head.

Demerre curbed his own. He knew that the boy was capable of leaving the nest, without worrying about what might become of him.

While Jacob was giving one last stroke of the razor to Lescalopier, whose turn had come, the populace was uttering loud cries. The exhibition of the condemned was beginning. But it was not bankrupts who were the cause of it; one of them was a very young man.

To begin with, the King of Ribauds mounted a platform. He had a long beard and was clad in a long black woolen robe. He was Master Gonin's cousin, the famous juggler; it had been the prize of his good offices. Étienne Mustau held in his hand a parchment, which he unrolled gravely, and recited in a resounding voice

"Oyez, knights, squires and all manner of people. In the name of Charles VI, King of France, the provost of Paris has ordered the exhibition in the pillory of Les Halles de Saint-Eustace, of Nicolas Maillet, convicted of having said in the open street that all the coins struck under this reign are of low title and false weight; the condemned will be exposed for two hours and will then receive twenty lashes on the bare shoulders, without interruption."

Without the halberds of the archers who were holding the people at bay, Mustau would have been pelted with mud with a few stones included. He continued: "The Provost of Paris has ordered in the second place the exhibition of Richard Carpalin, convicted of having insulted and threatened Monseigneur Louis de France, Duc d'Orléans, brother of the king. The condemned will be exposed for two hours in the pillory and then receive forty lashes to the bare shoulders, without interruption."

As the murmurs commenced to rise again, even more comminatory, the King of Ribauds hastened to issue the customary warning:

"I, Étienne Mustau, remind those present that it is forbidden to throw stones or raw apples at the condemned, on pain of prison. I have spoken."

Then he had the heads and hands of the patients passed through the holes in the mobile wheel, which was to compete its rotation every half an hour.

The crowd, splitting into groups, delivered itself to more or less hostile commentaries.

"Henchman of the Devil, it's you that we'd have pleasure in showering you with mud," said one spectator between his teeth, who appeared to summarize the general opinion.

The three merchants emerged from the barber's shop, formed a group and formulated their various sentiments.

They were talking about Carpalin.

"He must be a creditor of the Duc d'Orléans who ran out of patience," said Guérin-Bousseau.

"It's the Duc who ought to be there," sighed Bournichon.

"Well, personally," said Lescalopier, "I don't share your hatred. Monseigneur d'Orléans is an amiable prince. If he doesn't pay his debts, at least he looks the part. He's not like Monseigneur de Bourgogne. That one's not big spender, but what a costume! One might think him one of the kings of the fraternities who walk around festivals with fine clothes that they return in the evening."

"Well said," exclaimed young Jacob, who arrived at that point in the discussion.

"What does it have to do with you, child?" retorted Guérin-Boisseau; and he added, addressing Lescalopier. "I don't care about his good looks. What I prefer is good conduct. My man is Monseigneur de Bourgogne, who loves the people and who wouldn't pressure them for his pleasures if he were the master."

Jacob was about to riposte when Jehan Demerre arrived, who had come to satisfy his curiosity, having furbished his armor and his razors.

The attention of the merchants was then drawn to an itinerant monk, his satchel on his back, with a wrinkled face and a white beard, who was begging in a fashion to sow fear in the corner of a wood. He had drawn near to the pillory, and, having raised his eyes to the mobile wheel, he had not been able to dissimulate the satisfaction that the spectacle caused him to experience. His entire collapsed being stiffened, and a joyful fury blazed in his eyes, but he masked his joy rapidly. He lowered his head and resumed his role of beggar; he put his hands together forcefully and moved the lips hidden beneath his long beard, but the dilatation of his cheeks attested the movement. It was thus that he approached the barber's shop.

"The saintly man," said a fishmonger with compunction. "He's praying for the condemned."

XX. JEAN PETIT

For that earthly being whose name is unknown,
His eyes once lowered and almost unperceived,
Is a blazing beacon; he is a frightful demon
As black as the night, but is thought to be an elect.

That monk, who belonged to the Franciscan Order
and whose name was Jean Petit, was not a simple mendicant.[43] He was also a preacher of noisy renown. Quétif,
in his *Book of Preachers*, says of him: *Eloquens sed
ventosus*, a true tempest.[44] He preached in order to be
understood by all, especially the people. While Gerson
recommended sagacity, Petit preached the suppression

---

[43] The historical Jean Petit, or Jehan Parvus (c.1360-1411) was
a professor at the University of Paris, not a mendicant monk;
he became notorious for defending Jean *Sans Peur* against the
accusation that he had organized the assassination of Orléans,
on the grounds that the murder was legitimate tyrannicide.
Jean Petit could, of course, be translated as "Little John," and
that might well have influenced his transfiguration here. It was
the Romantic historian Augustin Thierry who popularized and
embellished the legend of the English outlaw Robin Hood in
France; another member of the *cénacles*. S. Henry Berthoud,
quoted Thierry at length when introducing Robin Hood as a
character into his historical romance "L'Ange de Williams"
(1934; tr. as William's Angel")
[44] Jacques Quétif (1618-1698) was a French Dominican com-
missioned to write a history of the order; the inclusion of Jean
Petit suggests that the latter was a Dominican, but that seems
uncertain; Quétif's *Scriptores ordinis preadicatrum* was published posthumously in 1719-21.

of tyrants, assassination. What tyrants? One alone was envisaged: the Duc d'Orléans. People wondered why he hated the prince so much; no one could divine his secret.

After the station before the pillory, Jean Petit had resumed his quest; when he entered the barber's shop the latter had just returned to his domicile, where a client was waiting. Jacob had preceded him.

"Brothers," said the monk, "Help the poor limbs of Jesus Christ who are in great weakness."

"Indeed, said a rather well-furred furrier, whom Jacob was about to shave, "if the other monks are as bony as this one, they won't be cooking in their juices come summer."

He gave him a maille as faded as an old liard, and worth as little.

"Personally," said Demerre, "I give alms in kind. Here's a livre of good soap to keep the limbs of Our Lord clean."

"May Saint François render it to you," replied Jean Petit, and passed on to another shop.

When the last client had quit the place, the barber said to his grandson: "We can close the door; no one else will come. Everyone will be at the princes' ceremony. Find a good spot to watch the procession pass by. I'll go to my post in the Rue Mauconseil; you go to the steps of Saint-Eustache, you'll have a better view. Oh. there's a denier for your midday meal."

"Thank you, Father." Silently, the young man said to himself: *I can do without a midday meal. I already have two deniers put aside; with this I can buy a good knife, which I can put in my belt, as gentlemen do.*

"But before running off," said the barber, who was putting on his uniform of the bourgeois militia, "help me to tie my centurion, and give me my helmet."

176

When that was done he departed proudly, making the iron of his halberd ring on the paving stones.

He smiled on seeing the mendicant monk stop near the theater of the Carefree Children, in front of which Coquillart, the actor charged with the parade, was sniffing the air, inhaling eloquence.

Coquillart was extracted from his reverie by the monk's patter: "Brother, help the poor limbs of Jesus Christ!"

"Indeed," said Coquillart, "is it appropriate that the Devil gives alms to God?"

"My brother, you're insulting yourself."

"Not at all! Isn't that how you talk in your sermons?"

"They're parables. But it's above all because you give your representations too close to the Lord's dwelling. Go further away, friend. But I'd like to say a word to your chief, the Prince of Fools. Where is he?"

"Here he comes now."

Gonin was about to climb the steps of the stage when the monk stopped him for his eternal refrain.

"Well," said the Prince of Fools, "has the quest been good today? The bag seems full, but the purse?"

"Alas, it only contains a few badly-marked deniers. We receive hardly any silver. The merchants only give the objects of their commerce, which is why the burden is heavy but the product thin."

"Yes, I understand. The baker gives bread, the draper cloth, the hosier a sock and the barber shaves the beard."

"Oh, that would infringe our rule; the barber gives a lump of soap.

"I'll do no less than all those good Christians. I'll give you a sample of my métier. I'll even leave you the choice.

"What do you mean?"

"What would you prefer, Father? A grimace or a feat of skill?"

"You're joking."

"That's my estate. Let's go for the skill."

Gonin rapidly enveloped the monk with his adroit hands, squeezed him a little as if to feel beneath his robe, and then, the exploration having finished, he said: "Hold out your hand Father."

"Oh! Oh!" said the monk, having done as he was told. "A Parisian sou."

"That's not all. Keep holding out the hand."

"Hmm! Hmm! Four porcupine écus, not eroded!"

"Keep holding it out."

"Three cheval francs! Ah, that's enough to lighten you of many sins."

"Past and future? Take it all without counting, then, or I have a lot on my conscience and I haven't finished yet."

The monk, whose hands were no longer sufficient, had lifted up his robe in order to collect the liberalities of the Prince of Fools, but when he wanted to empty them into his purse he found that it was no longer there.

"I see what you lack," said Gonin, "And I don't want to do things by halves. Here's the desired purse."

"Oh, Master Rogue, you've played with me."

"I warned you, Father."

"With such tricks you'll go straight to that edifice over there."

"The pillory is a theater like any other, the finest frame for grimaces that can be imagined. The jutting

178

heads have a grotesque effect, which gave our architects the idea for mascarons. But mine will never be shown there."

"Corbleu!" cried the monk—and then repressed the oath, which might have betrayed his military antecedents. "Body of Christ! You merit that frame, however, but the protection of Madame la Reine is delaying your supreme caper on the gallows."

"From actor to puppet would be a fall."

"Bah! What does it matter when one dies whether one dies perpendicularly or horizontally?"

"You take the matter philosophically, Father; those aren't the words of a monk. What is your name?"

"My name in religion?"

"Yes, your theatrical name.

"Brother Sachet, of the Capuchin Order.

"And I'm the Prince of Fools, but my name is Gonin. And yours?"

"Jean Petit."

"Jean Petit! I suspected as much. Furious in the pulpit, fundamentally an orator of intelligence. Why so furious?"

"Because I love to hate and I want to communicate my hatred to my listeners."

Jean Petit had thrown his hood backwards and showed a creviced face illuminated by glittering eyes.

"Yes, yes, I know, you detest Orléans profoundly," said Gonin. *To himself, he added: There's one whom nature has made up in a fine fashion. What a mask to borrow for one of our mysteries!*

Gonin changed masks four times in certain mysteries, from which has come the saying that the devil has four faces.

"Adieu, Father," he went on, aloud. "I'm obliged to quit you in order to prepare this evening's representation."

"But I'm not quitting you, my brother," said the monk, gravely. "I still have to talk to you."

When the Franciscan and the Prince of Fools were face to face on the stage, the eyes of the torture victims who were in the pillory, as if in the best places, squinted in amazement at that unexpected spectacle, the wheel having made a complete rotation.

"Friend, look in the direction of the pillory," said the monk. "Look at that blond head surmounted by a placard bearing the name Richard Carpalin."

"Indeed," replied Gonin, "Carpalin! I remember that name. Can that be the son of that grotesque individual who would have had so much success in my theater, and whose wife the Duc d'Orléans abducted? That's the progeniture of the ex-Sire de Cauny for sure; the young man can't be more than fifteen years old. What brought him here?"

"Vengeance," said the monk, in a muffled voice. "The Carpaulin you knew is dead. His wife has been abducted for a second time. He wanted to throw her out for having given him a child that couldn't be his, but he changed his mind, and that simple man, inspired by the spirit of vengeance, raised the child, Orleans' bastard, in the hatred of the latter. Isn't that a fine comedy, Prince of Fools: the son armed against the father? Richard Carpalin is, indeed, only fifteen years old, but he has been raised harshly and is the equal of a man for strength and decision. But he hasn't been able to contain himself, and has only been condemned for insulting the brother of the king. Let's be patient!"

"Father, I understand your regret in seeing him punished so severely for so little; but I wonder what you can want of me?"

"This: I know how much credit you have with Madame la Reine and Monseigneur de Bourgogne, who appears irreconcilable, but who is reconciling. It's uniquely a matter, for the moment, of the protection of Madame la Reine, to get that young man out of the hands of Messire the provost, in order that he can fulfill the sacred mission with which his father has charged him...the man he believes to be his father."

"But it's a pact with the Devil—for I'm the Devil—that you're proposing to me."

"I know."

"Like him, I have need of souls."

"I know," said the monk, energetically.

"So be it, I'll help you, Father. But an order from the queen will arrive too late to save him from the fustigation."

"Oh, it's not necessary that it arrives before. The whip is a marvelous stimulant."

"There's Christian charity!"

"Can I count on you, Prince of Fools?"

"Yes, certainly, since I have need of you."

"That's agreed, Adieu, my brother."

"Adieu, my friend."

Gonin, went into his arcana and the monk went down the steps. After having replaced his hood, he traversed a mass of curious people who had quit the pillory for the stage, and to enjoy the original prologue of a Franciscan in dialogue with the Prince of Fools in front of the theater of the Carefree Children.

The buffoon Coquillart, who was sitting discreetly to one side, stood up in order to begin his patter. He commenced with a song.

When I drink the wine of Beaune,
If you knew what I see,
If you knew what I believe...
Paris and its white houses
Seem to be a flock of sheep
And he bells are the shepherds
Who conduct them to the plain,
  Drink to the Seine!
But next to the water, what danger!
Three wolves are there to steal them,
Three wolves are there to eat them.
In the isle in the middle of the Palace,
One the banks the two Châtelets.

"It's good, that song," said Guérin-Boisseau, who was idling in front of the stage.

"We know what it signifies!" added Bournichon.

"Personally," said Lescalopier, "I think it's you two who are putting malice into it."

Another onlooker, who looked like a provincial, muttered timidly: "I don't understand; what does he mean with his song?"

"He's from Beauce, that one," yapped a gamin. "On your way!"

The crowd welcomed that gibe with noisy laughter.

"Silence!" said Coquillard, suddenly. "The Prince of Fools is going to speak in person."

In fact, the people's fool, not the king's, got ready to make himself heard.

XXI. BOURGOGNE AND ORLÉANS

If kings are cousins, people, you are brothers;
Peoples, liberty is the only divine right!

A great silence had fallen, in order not to miss a word from Master Gonin, who rarely deigned address the public himself from the height of the stage.

"People of Paris and elsewhere, if there are any here," clamored the powerful voice that had made the immense hall of the Château de Beauté resound, "The troupe of the Carefree Children, formed by me, the Prince of Fools, duly authorized by the king, our master, in order to perform farces, satires, devilries and moralities in the marketplace of the beautiful city of Paris, will give you this evening, at three o'clock in the afternoon, a representation of *The Martyrdom of Saint Eustache*, in which God the Father will appear in new clothes. Jérôme Coquillart, here present, will replace me in the role of Lucifer, obliged as I am to go to dinner at the Hôtel Saint-Pol.

At that moment a deafening music burst forth of cymbals, little bells and tambours.

When the racket had ceased, Gonin finished the announcement:

"That play will be followed by *The Long-Sought Peace*, which will accommodate Ludovic, a gentleman of Orléans, with Jeannot, a landowner of Bourgogne; under the form of a communion, they will share...a forgetfulness.

The music burst forth again, covering the laughter of the populace.

"I hope that such an impertinence will not be tolerated!" said Lescalopier to his two friends. "Where are we going if respect for princes is allowed to decline?"

"My opinion is that a good lesson should be given to Orléans," replied Bournichon.

"Mine too," added Guérin-Boisseau.

The Prince of Fools had not finished.

"Between the mystery and the farce," he said, "the dance of the Mataquins will be performed; then Jérôme Coquillart will recite a lay of my composition touching the deeds of the valiant archer Guillaume Tell, who slew the tyrant Gessler exactly a hundred years ago. I shall conclude, people of Paris and elsewhere, by begging you not to launch peas with blowpipes at God the Father, nor at his companions. It disturbs their playing. So, be chic…peas"

The laughter burst forth again, quickly drowned out by the heavy and implacable symphony.

"Who was this Gessler?" Bournichon asked Guérin-Boisseau.

"Doubtless something like our Duc d'Orléans," the latter replied.

"He was a person," Lescalopier said, "who had his apples picked by crossbow bolts, and who never missed you if you missed them."

In the meantime, Master Gonin descended from the stage and went to find Étienne Mustau at the foot of the pillory.

"Cousin," he said "I'd like to liberate that young fellow up there."

"One of your men?" asked the King of Ribauds."

"Future."

"You'd like to spare him the lash?"

"Exactly."

"Impossible! All the populace whom your parade attracted and who turned theater was ready to lapidate me when I put the carcan on Carpalin, but they'll bray like a legion of donkeys in rut if I deprive them of the advertised forty lashes.

"Worthy populace! It's necessary, however, that I snatch away their prey."

"How?"

"I've found a means; the Duc de Bourgogne could save the condemned man, could he not?"

"Undoubtedly."

"Well, he'll pass this way today to go to the ceremony. I'll settle things with him. How much time do we have?"

"Half an hour."

"That's enough; all the more so as I can hear 'Vive Bourgogne!' being shouted in the distance."

It was, in fact, the Duc who was advancing.

He had just quit his house in the Rue Pavée-Saint-Sauveur (now the Rue du Petit-Lion), a veritable fortress of which nothing any longer remains but a stout quadrangular tower in which two scrapers and a lead wire sculpted in the middle of Gothic fleurons can be seen in the ogival cavity of one of the exterior bays.

The Duc de Bourgogne came forward, therefore, preceding the people of his retinue by a few paces. He was wearing a severe costume with no gold or silver embroidery. He was a black rider, mounted on a black horse. When he stopped and the immobility of the man and the horse was complete, one searched for the pedestal, which was all that the equestrian statue lacked. The people admired the solidity of his torso and the breadth of his shoulders.

"Noël! Vive Bourgogne!" cried the crowd. In its enthusiasm, it threatened to submerge him.

The duc was glad of this popularity; he was accustomed to say to his intimates: "These civilities are the foundations that will win me a capital."

He spotted Master Gonin approaching him.

"Ah! There's our joyful friend the Prince of Fools. How goes your theater, Master?"

"Badly, Monseigneur. The merry-maker of our troupe is presently in the pillory. See the face he's pulling."

What has he done to be condemned?"

"He permitted himself a joke at the expense of Monseigneur d'Orléans."

"That was a mistake."

"A great mistake, no doubt, but Monseigneur, on such a solemn day, all punishments ought to be remitted, and you know the custom; when the king passes before the place of torture, he grants mercy to a condemned man. The king being ill, it would be worthy of you, Monseigneur, who enjoys one of the prerogatives of royalty, to exercise it in a most princely fashion."

"Well said, Master Fool, and I want to do as much."

He ordered two of his officers, Montaudouin and Raoulet d'Actonville, to go and liberate the patients.

When the two officers came back, bringing the latter, Gonin said: "My merrymaker is named Richard Carpalin," introducing him.

"I believe I recognize the face of the other," said the Duc, indicating the man who had derided the coinage.

"It's Nicolas Maillet, the water-carrier who is stationed outside Monseigneur's house," said Raoulet d'Actonville.

"Well, let him return to his buckets, and you, return to your fools, Master," said the duc, delighted with his joke.[45]

The populace acclaimed him again and ran forward to touch his hand.

After that ovation, Jean *Sans Peur*, as he was called then, continued in his way, not without difficulty; the crowd surrounded him, and everyone wanted to have his share of the handshakes. It was necessary for his archers to disengage him.

Scarcely had he drawn away than fanfares were heard from the direction of the Hôtel de Bohême. The Duc d'Orléans had learned what was happening and, instead of going straight to the church, he was making a detour in order that he too might touch the populace, or rather brave them, for he knew that he was detested.

---

[45] The wordplay that relates *seaux* [buckets] to *sots* [fools] does not translate alas, nor is there any viable substitute.

XXII. THE PEOPLE OF PARIS
AND THE DUC D'ORLÉANS

The people subjugated by an ignoble brake
Gnaw it in silence of groan in vain,
But sometimes also, awakened by shame
Their wrath is terrible and their vengeance prompt.

While the Duc d'Orléans crossed the distance that separated him from the marketplace, Richard Carpalin was taken by Mustau to his cousin.

On the way, the son of Mariette d'Anghuien, shoved by the crowd, bumped into another young man, the son of Coline Demerre. The two young men seized one another by the throat.

"Bastard!" said Richard Carpalin.

"Bastard yourself!" riposted the other, threatening him with his knife.

They did not know that they were touching the truth so fraternally.

Gonin separated them, sniggering.

Jacob Demerre drew away, grumbling,

The King of Ribauds said to the other: "Thank Master Gonin for the grace that Monseigneur de Bourgogne accorded you, on his plea."

"Thank you, Master," exclaimed Richard Carpalin, "and believe in my eternal gratitude."

"Bah! Gratitude! A fine smoke!"

"Ask, and you will have deeds instead of words."

"Good!"

"However…"

"What?"

"On the condition that you do not hinder me in the vengeance that I have sworn to accomplish."

"On the contrary! But tell me, my friend, you're very young to have projects of vengeance in your head."

"I've had that word in my mind since I first heard words spoken."

"It's your father who taught it to you?"

"Yes."

"What about your mother?"

"I hardly knew her."

"Enough talk, for the moment. Follow me."

Gonin went into his theater, where Richard Carpalin was disposed to follow him, when a strident sound of trumpets was heard, and cries of "Vive d'Orléans!"

At the same moment, the young man found himself drawn away by a turbulent crowd, and, tossed by the ebb and flow, he went to fall, like a wreck, at the feet of a troop of archers commanded by Riblet, who was trying in vain to open a passage, crying: "Back, serfs!"

Around the archers, a band of children, who had been following them since the Hôtel de Bohème, were shouting with an evident white-hot enthusiasm: "Vive d'Orléans!"

The duc was dazzling. He was wearing a cloak of sky-blue velvet, braided with gold and embroidered with fleurs-de-lys in silver thread and a hood of garnet velvet whose white, pink and green plumes fell in cascades, mingling with his long curly hair, which framed a neck as white as a woman's, around which a necklace of large pals coiled like a serpent.. Added to those borrowed attractions, his natural beauty was further augmented by a radiant satisfaction. His large eyes were shining with a flame ignited by some new infatuation. He had the calm of insouciance in the midst of the hostile populace.

The seigneurs of his retinue were also streaming with gold and silver.

"Since one can't speak to him at his home," said Bournichon to Guérin-Boisseau, "I'm going to address my request to him here."

"I'll support you, friend," relied the latter.

"Do you think so?" said Lescalopier. "What are your miserable affairs compared to the affairs of State that must occupy him."

His intervention was in vain. Bournichon went forward, accompanied by Guérin-Boiseau.

"Monseigneur," he shouted, "your officers are ruining us…and refusing to pay what they owe…and to have us paid what you owe us!"

"What is that serf singing?" asked d'Orléans.

"Here's another serf ready to sing you the same song," cried Guérin-Boisseau in his turn, "And here's a friend who could make a chorus," he added, pointing at Lescalopier, who was hiding in the crowd

He found other creditors there who, encouraged and challenged, came to replace the fugitive, uttering frightful clamors

"Hola! Riblet! Hola! Sergeant-at-arms, hasten to charge all that rabble!" cried d'Orléans, "And you Savoisy, dispatch your pages!"

"Alas," sighed the chamberlain, "Since the edict of the Parlement, I no longer have any pages."

As the menacing demands gathered pace, the duc went on, ironically. "Come on, peace! I've thought of you. You're all included in my testament."

"Then we'll soon be paid!" howled a species of Goliath in the costume of a butcher.

Seizing the bridle of Orléans' horse, he was threatening the duc with a cleaver when he collapsed heavily, stabbed in the lower abdomen by a knife himself.

The person who had struck him was none other than Jacob, but as he brandished his knife triumphantly another young man ran at him in order to snatch it from him and to strike the duc. That was Richard Carpalin.

Jacob tried to free himself, but he could not prevent his adversary from raising his weapon—except that the latter could not break the circle that had formed around him.

"By the dear God!" sad the Duc d'Orléans. "But for that child I'd be slain. Take him on your rump, Riblet; you'll introduce him to me when I return to the house."

"Yes, Monseigneur." And Riblet added, as he hoisted the child up: "Why, it's Jacob!"

"You know him?"

"He's the son of Coline Demerre, Monseigneur."

Orléans shuddered, and said in a pensive tone: "I recommend you to be doubly careful of him, Riblet."

The crowd was still growling and hurling insults, but as reinforcements could her heard arriving, the duc confronted the storm.

"Out of the way, serfs, or my men-at-arms and I will pass over your bodies!"

The popular mass divided in order to let the duc and his retinue pass.

Orléans suddenly noticed a young fellow who was brandishing a dagger and darting a gaze charged with imprecations at him from the height of Master Gonin's stage.

"Who's that enraged little devil?" he asked.

"The one who snatched the knife with which I'd killed the man from me, in order to kill you," said Jacob.

191

"Hola, little assassin, who are you, then?" asked Orléans, raising his voice.

"I'm the son of Mariette d'Anghuien," replied Richard Carpalin, in a quivering voice.

The duc had a sort of vertigo; he let the bridle of his horse escape, and then seized it again swiftly.

"My two bastards!" he murmured. "One wants to kill me, the other to defend me…their mothers would have been in accord. Then, with a gesture of command, he said: "Let's go, Messieurs, it's time for the ceremony."

In fact, midday was chiming at Saint-Eustache, and the ceremony had been arranged for midday.

XXIII. RICHARD AND JACOB

They extended their hands, embraced and wept,
But their gazes, reciprocally, insulted one another.

From the day when the scepter of Charles VI had fallen into the hands of Isabeau de Bavière and Louis d'Orléans, the apartments of the Hôtel Saint-Pol had been delivered to Italian artists, painters and sculptors. They had become a marvel of good taste, and in order to operate that metamorphoses, the duc had committed follies. The masons had received three Parisian sols pr day, the decorators six livres a month, the painters and sculptors fifteen, and the director of works twenty-five. That was then the height of prodigality.

The hall in which we have seen Charles VI hold his council, which had nothing regal about it, had been subjected to modifications that permitted a theater to be erected there on occasion. People came to set it up in order to celebrate the reconciliation of the two cousins. Gonin was at his post, hailing the men of his troupe.

"Hola, bastard of Phoebus Apollo, are we complete? On, two, three, four, five, six, me who beats the measure, seven…we'll be eight with our new recruit, who will have the appearance of blowing into his bagpipe but will abstain, for good reason.." He addressed the person in question directly: My young friend, pull down your fiddler's hood a little more; although I flatter myself that I've made you up so as to render the Richard Carpalin of the pillory unrecognizable, it's necessary not to neglect any precaution.

"Shall I sing, Master?" interjected the tenor of the Carefree Children.

"Perhaps, but you'll wait until you're begged and you'll sing something by Louis d'Orléans; that will do well. Now, all climb up on stage, to be ready for the first signal..."

Richard was about to install himself too when Gonin stopped him.

"Sit down next to me and let's chat while waiting for the arrival of the princes. First of all, don't think that, if I'm serving you in what you call your mission, it's because I approve of it. It's only because it enters into the plan I've formed. So I'll warn you when you have to go to speak to the Duc de Bourgogne and you'll tell him what we agreed. Now, let's get back to your story. So, it was in Coutras in Aquitaine, you told me, that your father took refuge?"

"Yes, Master; and he lived there by copying manuscripts."

"And it's from there that the Duc d'Orléans had your mother abducted, a conquest easier for him than that of Bordeaux?"

"Yes; my father, whom I hadn't seen for several years, had me come precipitately to Montpelier, where I studied, and made me swear to avenge the family of the outraged family in the blood of the abductor. 'I wouldn't charge you with this care,' he added, 'if privations and suffering hadn't robbed me of all strength; in a few days, I shall be no more. I'm counting on you.' I wanted to throw myself into his arms, but he stopped me with s gesture."

"That's strange. Before departing for Montpellier, did he testify any affection for you?"

"None."

"He was intent, however, in making a scholar of you?"

"That wasn't him; it was my mother. She counted, when my studies were complete, on sending me to Paris, where I was sure to succeed."

"Hmm. Knowledge isn't sufficient; it doesn't even count for anything. It's necessary to be of an extraction other than yours…to be at least the bastard of some seigneur."

Gonin pronounced the word "bastard" without appearing to want to make an allusion. Richard did not pay any heed to it.

"So I don't have any hope of arriving?" he said.

"If you had money, you might arrive at a fortune. Have you any?"

"No."

"It's necessary, then, to fall back on the two careers open to you: the Church and crime, a valve and a sewer. Monk or thief, choose! Who knows? You might rise to the top. A cobbler from Troyes had lately been seen to become Pope of Rome,[46] and at the present time the King of Argot is a legless cripple."

"Oh, Master, what a comparison!"

"My friend, I've warned you that in entering among us, it's necessary to make a *tabula rasa* of your brain, to deposit at our door, at the corner of the step, all the false ideas and stupid prejudices of your education. After that deballasting you'll have a clear mind and a clear eye. From the stage where you are, and from where the spectators will be the spectacle for you, you'll discover the truth of things; you'll see all the springs move that, ac-

---

[46] Pope Urban IV, elected in 1261, was formerly Jacques Pantaléon, the son of a cobbler from Troyes.

cording to the Greek Lucian, animate the thundering Jupiter that the people worship. You'll witness one scene in the long farce that will be played before you, and will be a day in history…I'll explain it to you like a faithful prologue."

Scarcely had he finished speaking than the trumpets sounded. There was a great noise in the courtyard of the Hôtel Saint-Pol, in which were mingled that clanking and clinking of armor, the snorting of horses, the cries of varlets and pages, the barking of greyhounds and the clamors of the populace. It was the princes coming back from the ceremony of the accolade.

Gonin and Richard hastened to mount the stage, and the musicians saluted with a symphony the entrance of the reconciled pair, holding hands. After them came the three ducs, their uncles, followed by all the nobles and wise men who had counseled a reconciliation in order to put an end to divisions of which the English had profited in order to extend their invasions.

The populace and the bourgeois had not only silenced their hatred but uttered joyous acclamations again on seeing the two enemies, having become friends, cross the distance that separated the church from the Hôtel Saint-Pol, mounted on the same horse, alternating in front and behind, with arms circling the midriff, taking turns to harangue the multitude at each station, in order that there should be parity between them. With an enthusiasm disengaged from the irony that Gonin had put into the two appellations, the crowd, as if the Prince of Fools' play, had shouted at the top of their voices: "Vive Jeannot! Vive Ludovic!"

While the two princes laughed at that familiar testimony of sympathy, a laughter that had gained all their retinue, from the most qualified seigneur to Riblet and the men-at-arms, young Jacob, still on the rump behind Riblet, saluted the crowd like a princeling.

When night fell, the illumination ordered by the provost of Paris took place with a perfect uniformity throughout the city. By the glow of candles lighted in all the windows, the people made merry, dancing and singing until dawn, not without drinking. By dint of clinking glasses, bodies collided, people were jostled and thumped. Many were to retain painful memories of the celebration.

The Ducs de Bourgogne and d'Orléans, harassed in their peregrination through the city and their joint ride, had let themselves fall into two gothic armchairs, abandoned a moment before by Master Gonin and Richard Carpalin.

They had suffered above all from a stifling heat complicated by whirlwinds of dist, so they did honor to the horns of ambered and musked hypocras that varlets presented to them on silver trays.

In the meantime, the Price of Fools' musicians executed their symphony.

XXIV. THE PAGE

A child, full of health, hope and years,
Without regret does the past or fear for the future,
Sees a beautiful destiny opening one morning,
Which the evening will wither.

The scene announced to Richard by Master Gonin did not take long to unfold.

"Cousin," said the black prince to the prince gilded and illuminated like an image of Saint Georges. I was sorry to hear what happened to you as you passed through the marketplace."

"Oh, mere trivia!" replied Orléans. "Merchants that my officers had forgotten to pay."

"Those poor people ought, however, to be paid…custom becomes right; it's true that the right in question isn't found in Charlemagne's *Capitulaires*; people had morals in that court!"

"Are you sure of that, Cousin? Nithard—a contemporary, and furthermore a grandson of Charlemagne, since he was the son of his daughter Berthe, secretly married to Angelbert—recounts that two of the daughters of that monarch, two of his aunts, who had embraced the religious life, scandalized the court by their behavior. I could also cite you the historian Aumoin…"[47]

"Oh, I don't doubt your great knowledge. I admit everything you say about the past, but let's get back to

---

[47] The references are to the Frankish historian Nithard (c.795-844) and the chronicler Aumoin de Fleury (c.960-c.1010)

what concerns you; it's certain that you were in some danger."

"Let's leave that, nephew de Bourgogne," said the Duc de Berry. "There's nothing there but reason to whip a villein; the proof is the acclamations with which the populace saluted both of you just now."

"However," Jean persisted, "it's said that without the intervention of a child..."

"By the way, Chamberlain Savoisy," said Orléans, "I want that child to be attached to me person as a page, in spite of the regulation."

"It's already done, Monseigneur!" And he went to fetch Jacob from the back of the room, in the costume of a page.

"Truly," said Orléans, "one might think he had the habit of it. He's charming, in good grace,"

He caressed his cheeks with the back of his hand; he would have kissed him had he not been surrounded by witnesses who were already committing the sin of slander, including Hugues de Guisay, who was reminding a neighbor of the appearance of Coline Demerre at the court of amour.[48]

"You won't quit me any longer, little page; you'll serve at my table."

"Oh! I'm very glad," replied Jacob, proud and ecstatic.

"There's an adolescent," said Jean, "Who would be killed for you if the occasion arose, and today's adventure, cousin, might be renewed and aggravated."

Orléans, stung to the quick by that obstinacy, retorted loudly: "I admit that I have done nothing to please the

---

[48] The author has apparently forgotten that Hugues de Guisay died in the fire at the tragic ball.

rabble; I have never been seen giving handshakes to butchers or curriers and offing my cheek to the garlic-flavored kisses of the women of market. Pooh! That's where the insolence and rebellion of the people comes from. I've composed a fable on the subject that you can meditate; it's a matter of a knight who extends his hand to a peasant; the peasant commences by kissing it, then he shakes it in his own, then he pulls it rudely, and he finally throws the knight to the ground."

"An excellent subject for a fable," said Hugues de Guisay.

"I'll throw you there one day, with the peasant's hand that you despise," murmured the Duc de Bour-gogne.

The Ducs d'Anjou, de Berry and de Bourbon, want-ing to interrupt that dialogue, which was threatening to take a bad turn, stood up, pretexting their appetite.

Orléans made a sign and the curtains at the back opened, revealing a laden table, on which were erected bizarre monuments in patisserie, surrounded by flowers. The five ducs took their places behind it, and behind each of them stood one of the gentlemen attached to his person: Raoulet d'Actonville behind the Duc de Bour-gogne, and behind Anjou, Berry and Bourbon, Sourdis, Montaudouin and Tuillières; as for Orléans, Jacob filled the agreed office for him.

It was Charles de Savoisy, the king's chamberlain, who was responsible for the organization of the feast.

Trumpets preceded the numerous varlets who circu-lated around the table, carrying ewes and silver platters; their fanfares, which resounded at intervals, covered the eternal symphony, which had resumed its course.

Bourgogne and Orléans, sitting side by side, were prodigal with simulated graciousness, as to which of the two would not be served first. The majority of their partisans seemed edified by it, but there were some whom the game did not deceive.

"Hmm!" whispered Guisay in the ear of Tuillières, whom he knew to be in favor of the king's brother, "I hope the Monsieur d'Orléans will not allow himself to be taken in by Jeannot's grimaces."

"You can be sure of that, Sire Hugues; after supper he will not fail to inundate his hands with perfume in order to purify him from that abject contact, soiled by the populace."

"Ah! When will the moment come to chastise the insolence of the leader and his retinue?" murmured Raoulet d'Actonville, who had missed nothing of Tuillières' response.

XXV. THE BALLAD

Orléans, possessed of a feminine sensibility and the temperament of a poet, was under the spell of the flowers with which the table was strewn; but multiplied swigs of wine ended up extracting him from that reverie.

"Chamberlain," he said, "is the Prince of Fools not present?"

"He is on his stage, Monseigneur, in the midst of his musicians."

"Have him come down, please."

At a sign from the chamberlain, Gonin presented himself before the duc with an embarrassment that was quite real. He recalled the scene in the Château de Beauté, and since that day he had always feared being recognized, although he was heavily made-up.

"It appears droll," said the duc, "that you permit allegories in our regard…"

"Bah, cousin!" Bourgogne hastened to say, playing the good prince. "Pardon him, for the wit that he puts into it."

"So I shall, but on one condition."

"What is that, Monseigneur?" asked Gonin.

"It's that you allow me to appreciate the prettiest of your ballerinas, who are said to be the flower of beauty."

"Almost a rosebud."

"Only almost?"

"She has an excuse; her homeland being very warm."

"Which?"

"Andalusia, Monseigneur."

To himself, Gonin said: *An Andalusia of the Rue Glatigny!* The Rue de Glatigny was qualified by an old and naïve chronicler as "a street where there are prostitutes."

"Good," added Orléans. "We'll talk about it again. Now, after the ballerina, let's pass on to the players. You will take care, Prince of Fools, to have them all at the disposition of the chamberlain tomorrow, who will pass them in review. You understand, Savoisy?"

"Perfectly, Monseigneur."

"I don't understand," said Gonin.

"It isn't necessary for you to understand."

"Perhaps it's as well that I don't understand."

"You reason more than is reasonable, Prince of Fools; that's enough, it's too much."

Gonin bowed and returned to his stage.

"Cousin Bourgogne," said Orléans, "it's a long time since Madame Marguerite de Hainaut came to Paris...with her graces and intelligence she was the ornament of the court while you were making war against the infidels."

"She prefers retreat and is more comfortable in her duchy," replied Jean, scarcely containing himself.

"It's strange, this distaste for Paris, which she did not have while you were a prisoner of the Turks."

Jean was about to explode when the Duc de Berry intervened.

"Handsome nephews, you're not eating; these are, however, the most exquisite golden plovers."

While both of them accepted the proffered dish, he said in a low voice to the Ducs de Bourbon and d'Anjou: "The reconciliation will not be of long duration if we don't mingle in the conversation." Aloud, he added: "Is it true, Duc Jean, that the Turks make use of a certain beverage as black as ink, which they call coffee?"

"Is it true," added the Duc de Bourbon for his part, "that they shave their heads and only allow a single hank of hair to grow, by which the angel of death has to seize them in order to transport them to Mahomet's paradise?"

"Is it true, asked Anjou, again, "that they never drink wine?"

To the first two questions Bourgogne contented himself with an affirmative nod of the head; to the third he replied: "Never, in which they're wiser than us."

"Wiser?" exclaimed Orléans, ironically. "But do they not also have several wives, and imprison them in a redoubt they all a seraglio?"

"It's not for you to throw stones into their seraglio, you who can be reproached for your 'Val d'amour.'"

"An invention, cousin, of your friends the butchers and tanners…it diverts simpletons in the barbers' shops."

"And your gallant escapades, are they fanciful tales? Is your modesty alarmed by the conquests that are attributed to you?"

"Not at all, Cousin Jeannot, as the Prince of Fools calls you. Your cousin Ludovic has encountered few ladies whom he has solicited amour in vain, but he takes no vanity from it, remembering the dictum of an old fable: *You are, were, or will be what fate or will dictates*."

"You're cruel to the weaker sex, Cousin Ludovic— unjustly cruel, I will add. Virtue doesn't run the streets, agreed; but there are still numerous examples."

"Hmm! That's what Master Gonin says on his stage. Only he adds that it is…pardon, cousin, the opinion of simple minds, which are also the more numerous."

"Master Gonin is a conjurer. He's only an authority on that point for you because you've made the decision to judge woman by women of the sort whose full-length portraits are arranged by date in the gallery of your Hôtel de Brehaigne. It's necessary to add, to be exact, in the costume of the terrestrial paradise. When will you show us that gallery, cousin?"

"When the moon eclipses the sun."

"Why so much mystery?"

"Because I fear interested eyes."

"Mine, I hope, are not of that number?"

"Handsome cousin, you will always be among the exceptions."

"Wretch!" growled Bourgogne, kneading the hilt of his sword with rage.

"Serve the spices and the nectar!" cried Berry, to interrupt the scene,

Then all the pages and varlets hastened to offer the guests aniseed cakes and bottles filled with rosé wine, furnished by the fine province of Champagne, united with the realm of France after the mirage of Philippe le Bel with Jeanne de Navarre. The wine fizzed in the glasses, sparkling, and made the most taciturn chatty. Even Bourgogne was subject to the charms of the draughts to which the king's uncles had invited him in order to drown his rancor.

Crowned with flowers like an Athenian of the time of Anacreon or a Roman of the decadence, Orléans suddenly rose to his feet, emptied his golden cup and cried gaily: "This feast is delectable, but it lacks its soul: a troubadour."

"The feast is complete," said the Seigneur de Boisbourdon. "Does it not possess the Prince of Troubadours?"

"Flatterer!"

"Renown is also a flatterer, which celebrates your talent as a poet with her hundred voices. Oh, if I dared, Monseigneur..."

"What would you do?"

"I would address a request to you that would certainly be applauded by all the seigneurs surrounding me."

"What request?"

"I would beg you, Monseigneur, to recite us one of the rhymed works, ballads or virelays, that you make and say so beautifully."

"Well, I'm a good prince, I'm ready to fulfill the role of troubadour; but first, page, go fetch from the next room a casket that I had brought in anticipation of what might happen."

Jacob hastened to obey, and Orléans took sheets of paper from the casket covered in his handwriting. He made a choice and consulted Charles de Savoisy, who begged him in a whisper to abstain.

"Bah!" replied Orléans, in the same tone. "He has a head too hard for that to penetrate it. "Monseigneur," he added, raising his voice, "I'll recite you a ballad on a lady of high birth whose name I shall not say, but to make full value of it I need an accompanist. Savoisy, have Gonin come."

The Prince of Fools hastened. Orléans asked him whether he knew his ballad commencing with the words "My darling in every place is proclaimed."

"Perfectly," replied Gonin. "Not only do I know it, but I've set it to music, like all Your Seigneurie's works."

"In truth?"

"I'm ready to give you the proof of it."

"I'll furnish you with the opportunity soon." Then he said to Gonin, smiling: "Let's not forget the serious thing you mentioned to me."

"What, Monseigneur?"

"The lovely ballerina that you were to present to me."

"Yes—when do you desire her?"

"Tomorrow, at midday, in my Château de Beauté. Do you know where it is?"

"No, I don't know," said Gonin, audaciously.

"Between the Bois de Vincennes and Nogent. Now, to the music!"

While the Prince of Fools returned to his stage, a flash of philosophy traversed his mind. *Everything in this world is naught but comedy*, he said to himself; *a little while ago I was playing my role with a monk, now it's with a king's son. Nothing is true but theatrical costumes; I call Aristophanes and Plautus as witnesses! The farce worthy of scorn is history!*

Emerging from his lyrical reverie, Gonin gave the order to his musicians to get ready to play the tune of the famous ballad. The latter tuned their instruments and, at a sign from their leader, launched into the piece. Seizing the key in flight, Orléans adapted his first strophe to it.

My darling in every place is proclaimed
As a beautiful and noble of blood;
By the name of a flower she is named,
And lady of a powerful lord,
Whom great honor and renown
Acquits in the land of the Crescent...

The allusion was flagrant; the friends of the poet prince laughed surreptitiously or quivered at the hatred that was amassed against him. His uncles were in despair at the insensate prank. As for the Duc de Bourgogne, Raoulet d'Actonville, fearing a precipitate explosion, forced him to calm down and retained his arm

With the intoxication of the poet, Orléans continued, madly.

Weary, the fine sire scarcely knows
That in the time he was at war
She listened to my gentle pleas
And one evening my straying hand
Undid her gilded belt
And loosened her blonde hair.

The diversity of the impressions of the audience is understandable.

"These verses are yours?" said Jean *Sans Peur* to Orléans, in a dull voice.

"Yes, Duc, and that's not all."

"Ah! Let's see!" added Bourgogne, still quivering.

Then he whispered in the ear of Raoulet d'Actonville, who was making a sign to him with one hand to be patient, and agitating a dagger in its sheath with the other: "I'll make your fortune if..."

"It's done, Monseigneur."

Orléans finished, without blinking:

Ah, beautiful flower, in my distress,
Since then I've claimed you in vain,
And I have no other pleasure
Than your portrait made by my hand.

"And that portrait figures in the secret cabinet of the Hôtel de Brehaigne?" asked Bourgogne, his eyes bloodshot.

"Yes, Duc, and as perfect as the lines you've just heard," replied Orléans, with an imperturbable nonchalance. "Modesty is the virtue of the impotent."

"As patience is the virtue of donkeys," growled Jean *Sans Peur*, who was getting up to strike Orléans when a heart-rending scream, the cry of a wild beast, coming from behind a partition, burst forth and chilled the entire audience with fear.

The king had escaped from his prison and, pursued, was uttering veritable howls. He appeared on the threshold, like the specter of misery and hunger.

XXVI. THE VAL D'AMOUR

I was born in Eden under a bower of roses
In the first kiss of the first two lovers.
The sweetness of my voice extends over everything.

Have you ever stopped before a portrait by Holbein, representing harshly a naked body lying on a slab, stiff and motionless, the hair flat and straight, the belly collapsed, the skin green-tinted, a horrible thin, in truth? Well, the thing that suddenly appeared, and was named Charles VI, was even more frightful. That cadaver was upright, walking and howling.

The poor madman finally calmed down, and a little reason penetrated his skull.

"What light!" he sighed, extenuated. "What an abundantly served table! Why haven't I been invited, I who am dying of hunger?"

And, seized a fowl that was still entire, he fled into a corner, in order to bite into it gluttonously.

"Monsieur d'Orléans," said Jean *Sans Peur*, "this is your work. Oh, you will have a terrible account to settle one day."

"If anyone has an account to settle for the sad state of the king, it's God alone. Let him restore the health and reason that he took away, and there will no longer be any need to treat him as a being confined to the animal. He's nothing but a furious madman."

"Who is the traitor who speaks thus?" cried Charles, jumping as if he had felt a spur. "Mad? Yes, that's fatality! But furious? Why furious? Furious at the evil treatment I'm obliged to suffer."

"What did I say?" said Bourgogne, turning to Orléans. Then he addressed Charles VI. "Monseigneur le Roi, recover your senses and count on the loyal servants you will not lack."

"The king? Who says that I'm the king? It's necessary that everyone knows it and confesses it! There are still honest men in this palace. Yes, I'm the king. It's necessary that everyone testifies the respect that they owe me. Oh, I recall the terrible malady by which I was struck! I had lost my reason; but I've recovered it in spite of the dungeon in which I've been imprisoned. It's over!"

"You understand now," observed Bourgogne to Orléans.

The latter only replied to the king. "My brother," he cried in a tone of sincerity, "What a powerful subject of joy for all, and principally for the one who is so close to you. I want to go and thank Monsieur Saint Denys!"

"As do we," said the other three.

"Provided," added Berry, "that this light of reason doesn't disappear again!"

"But first," said Bourgogne, "take away those soiled and torn vestments; after that, we'll see to the intelligence. Master Jehan Coquerel has spoken to me of a young woman named Odette,[49] very expert in the art of

---

[49] Some chronicles record that in 1405 or thereabouts, the king was provided with a mistress, Odette de Champdivers, who resembled the queen, but they also allege that his marital relations continued; Isabeau's final pregnancy occurring in 1407, as in the present story (although the author has no difficulty accounting for that without involving the king). The chronicles also allege—contrary to the present story—that she was in the king's chamber when Orléans was assassinated on 23 November 1407.

caring for the sick; the care of the king can be confided to her if he falls back into melancholy."

"Well thought," said Berry.

"There is also a pleasant card game invented by a certain Pierre Gringonneur,[50] which is appropriate to cheering up the sick."

"I thank you, Jean de Bourgogne," said Charles. "You see that I recognize you. As for you, who say you are my brother...I also remember that you have abused my illness!"

"My brother, you're accusing me wrongly. I've been absent for a long time for matters of war, and your worthy wife..."

"My worthy wife? Oh yes, Isabelle—but where is she?"

"The queen," said the Duc de Berry, "has not yet got up from her latest childbirth."

"Childbirth! I knew nothing about it. May I know who has done her harm, and what child has come to me?"

"A son."

"Where is his father?"

Bourgogne bit his tongue in order not to name Orléans.

"I want to see this son," said the king. "I shall know."

---

[50] "Pierre Gringonneur" is credited by some sources as the originator of a supposedly Medieval Tarot deck, also known as the Charles VI Tarot, because of an assertion that they were presented to the king as a present in 1392. There is no reliable reference to their existence before the sixteenth century, but the deck in question still exists, held in the Bibliothèque Nationale.

"Sire, he died."

"He has done well. But dress me. Messieurs, let us occupy ourselves with affairs of State."

So saying, Charles VI, of whom it was said that he was the wisest man in the realm when he was not the maddest, resumed his royal bearing. He headed toward the apartments followed by the Ducs d'Anjou and de Bourbon and the gentlemen of his retinue,

There remained the Ducs de Berry, d'Orléans and Bourgogne, Raoulet d'Actonville and Jacob, not to mention Gonin and Richard Carpalin, who had let the musicians leave and had hidden in the darkest corner of their stage in order to witness the development of the comedy, or the historical drama.

"Alas," sighed Berry, "I'm greatly afraid that the king is only having a flash of sanity."

"I'd dearly like him to resume the burden of government, though," said Orléans

The king will have great difficulty restoring order to the finances," growled Bourgogne.

"You always look on the black side, my cousin. Let's see, would it not please you to call a truce to this ill humor with a game of dice?"

"I'd dread that in beating you I'd be accused of ruining the public treasury."

"Hmm! After the battle of Nicopolis, the Turk Bajazet qualified you as a bull. You don't spare the thrusts of your horns."

At that brutal insult, Jean *Sans Peur* made as if to run at Orléans again. Berry interposed himself once more.

"If my nephew Bourgogne doesn't want to play," he said, "he can distract himself in admiring the images with which Jean de Bruges has ornamented the romance of Renaud de Montauban, which is on that table." And he dragged Orleans into the next room, disposed as a gaming room.

The latter, followed by Jacob, escaped laterally and, after having deposited the manuscript of his poetry in the casket with which the page had come in quest of them, went into a subterranean tunnel that led to the Hôtel de Brehaigne, where the Val d'Amour was.

He arrived in the small and pretty apartment that Mariette d'Anghuien still occupied. Before entering the sanctuary where the only woman he had ever loved reposed on a bed of velvet, lace and silk, the prince ordered the page to make sure that no one penetrated the Val d'Amour by way of a door that led to his own apartments. He passed a silver chain around his neck, from which a silver whistle was suspended.

Jacob had been walking back and forth in the gallery for a little while when the desire of a curious child crossed his mind. As he had followed the prince, he had glimpsed, by the indecisive light of a lamp that was never extinguished, painted beauties that stimulated his youth. The boys of that time had the same temptations as those of today. Every time that his coming and going approached the Val d'Amour, Jacob advanced further in the temptation to see.

In the end, he infringed the order that he had been given to keep watch. He went in, and all the more-or-less veiled beauties gazed at him fixedly, seeming to say to him: "Bonjour, my little friend, come here so that I can kiss you on your fresh and rosy lips." And he went, and planted his lips on the portraits that seemed to him to be the most eloquent.

After that intoxication, a charm of a more delicate nature attracted him to a portrait of infinite tenderness, which appeared to be ashamed to be in that secret museum. He had a kind of revelation, looked more closely, and read on the upper part of the frame the name of Coline Demerre.

"Oh!" he exclaimed. "So it's true!"

Under the impact of that emotion, his knees buckled and he fell to the floor, inanimate.

When he came round, he was lying on a bed of repose, next to which a woman was standing, who was still beautiful. It was Mariette d'Anghuien, who was lavishing maternal cares upon him.

Did she not imagine that he was her son?

XXVII. THE BASTARD

When hatred comes to sit down next to a mortal,
"Choose between two evils," it says to him, "decide,
You have only two paths; it is shame or despair;
You have only two friends; it is crime or suicide."

Orléans had had a brief conversation with Mariette d'Anghuien, in which he had informed her of the presence of her son in Paris, and of their encounter, which might have been fatal for him. He had reassured her as to the outcome of the assassination attempt of which he had been the object and had promised to reunite them; hence the mistake that had just occurred.

While Charles VI was donning his royal costume in order to go and hold is plenary court in the State Council Chamber, Gonin, in the shadow of the stage, showed Richard the Duc de Bourgogne, motionless and pensive, and whispered in his ear:

"You see that man. A few hours ago he was the most fortunate and most triumphant seigneur in Christendom. He was cradled by golden dreams in the acclamations of the people. They were crying 'Vive Bourgogne!' and Orléans only collected murmurs, not to say insults, in his passage. Now the latter has let a few words fall from his mouth that have changed everything. He too has been acclaimed. That reversal has only increased the hatred that Bourgogne has for Orléans, and the ballad you have heard has added all the poisons of jealousy to it. It's at that dolorous point that it's necessary to strike. Follow my instructions, go straight to the Duc and find the means to speak to him about the Val d'Amour."

"Why don't you do it yourself?"

"Because I'm only a buffoon and I ought only to create laughter. You hate *the other*, as he does; stimulate your two hatreds together."

On that pressing invitation Richard descended from the stage and, without paying any attention to Raoulet d'Actonville, who was watching over his master and following him with his gaze, he drew slowly nearer to the duc, who resembled one of the stone knights sculpted on tombs and who, shaking off his torpor, started repeating:

And I have no other pleasure
Than your portrait made by my hand.

Then, violently agitated, Bourgogne clenched his fists and murmured: "Wretch!"

At the same moment, he perceived Richard.

"Monseigneur," said the latter, very emotionally.

"Who are you?"

"The man you liberated from the pillory today."

"What do you want?"

"Assistance against a high and powerful seigneur."

"Which?"

"Monseigneur d'Orléans."

"What is there in common between him and you?"

"There is my mother."

"Explain."

Richard told him about the flight of his father—the man he believed to be his father—the abduction of his mother and her sequestration. He had been to the Hôtel de Brehaigne in order to reclaim her from the duc himself, and he had been thrown out, told that the Hôtel de Brehaigne was not like the Hôtel d'Artois, which any

217

peasant could enter; and when he had protested, treating the duc as he merited, he had been tied up and delivered to the provost of Paris."

"You don't know, then, where your mother has been imprisoned?"

"Master Gonin, who knows, if not everything, almost everything, affirms to me that it is probably close to what he calls the Val..."

"The Val d'Amour! And you want to penetrate it?"

"Yes, Monseigneur."

"How?"

"Would you, Monseigneur, simply express the desire that at the fête that Monseigneur d'Orléans is due to give you tonight in his house, Master Gonin and his troupe will collaborate by means of their diversions. As I'm now part of the troupe..."

"Yes, but that's not all; what will you do then?"

"Master Gonin will furnish me the means. First of all, the habitude is, at the Hôtel de Brehaigne, to serve for the Prince of Fools and his troupe, for the preparations for their diversions, a portion of the gallery that neighbors the Val; furthermore, Master Gonin possesses, I don't know how, a key to the secret section of the house.."

"Well, we'll go together into that den, that Val d'Amour; you'll go where your filial duty tells you to go...and I'll satisfy my curiosity."

"Alas, Monseigneur, I fear that attention might be alerted if you're seen to get up and follow a path without issue."

"Have no fear," said Raoulet d'Actonville, intervening. "I'll foment a discord between Monseigneur de Bourgogne's men and Monseigneur d'Orléans' men, by the favor of which anything will be possible."

"Let it be done thus," said Bourgogne, getting up.[51]

"I'll obey you, Monseigneur," replied Richard, bowing.

The duc headed for the gaming room; there was an argument there that was about to come to blows.

At the moment when Richard rejoined Gonin, Raoulet said to his master: "That's a boy of whom I won't lose sight. His employment is found; the chastisement will be complete."

Jean *Sans Peur* made no reply and went into the gaming room, where the tumult appeared to be calming down.

---

[51] Presumably, the scene indicated by this plan was supposed to take up a section of text following the point at which the king falls asleep in the fragmentary text making up the next chapter, which was not written.

XXVIII. THE CARD GAME

When he died he didn't have a liard;
And as losing was customary for him,
If he has reached Paradise, I presume
He must owe it to a great stroke of luck.

Before Charles VI only the game of dice was known, the origin of which is unknown, so distant is it. The brother of Saint Louis is cited among the most curious players. Du Guesclin lost at that game everything he possessed, and the conqueror of the English would have died on a bed of straw but for the liberalities of Charles V.

Louis d'Orléans loved gambling as passionately as he loved women. Before the madness of Charles VI that was what had drained his brother dry.

When the game of cards was invented for the amusement of the king, it replaced the game of dice. It was a fad that became a fury. The Hôtel de Nesles, transformed into a gambling den, was often the theater of bloody battles.

As we have just seen, people could even come to blows in the king's palace. It was his uncles who put a stop to the scandal.

Jean *Sans Peur* crossed the room and went out, after having taken his leave of the players.

Not far away, Charles VI, who had put on his richest clothes, oppressed by a laborious digestion explicable by the voracity with which he had calmed his hunger, was asleep on a chair that served him as a throne.

That reparative sleep was prolonged until dawn.

When he woke up, Charles VI was free and disposed. He had recovered the plenitude of his reason. He was preparing to go and hold his council while his brother was thinking about going to the Château de Beauté to receive from the hands of Gonin the young woman he had ordered the latter to bring him. Before then, he had to go to Vincennes in order to contain news of the queen. He had relieved of his guard his page Jacob, who refrained careful from confessing the cause of his faint, and who mounted a horse in order to follow the prince with a filial enthusiasm.

Orléans was no longer thinking about his brother, in whom he had already seen flashes of lucidity that only lasted a few minutes, and were not worth the trouble of being taken into account.

XXIX. THE KING

Decked with his royal insignia. Charles VI made his entrance to the State Council Chamber with a majesty that contrasted singularly with his attitude of the previous evening. The queen, scarcely recovered from her childbirth, had come to join him in al haste. She sat down beside her husband on a seat slightly less elevated than the royal seat; two maids of honor stood behind her, and behind them, two other ladies had taken their places on stools.

Around an immense oval table were arranged, after the king, the Ducs de Berry, d'Anjou and de Bourbon, then the Duc de Bourgogne; one place remained empty, that of the Duc d'Orléans; a group of seigneurs of both parties completed the assembly.

"Peace and salutations to all," said Charles VI, with a slight inclination of the head. Sit down and tell us where the affairs of our kingdom are."

"Sire," said the Duc de Berry, "the kingdom is tranquil. No more revolts, no more wars. The English have disappeared, commerce is reborn; but money is still scarce."

"How can money be scarce if commerce is reborn? And the English have a singular fashion of disappearing while still encroaching. Do you have the same sentiment, cousin Bourgogne?"

"Sire," replied the latter, "this is what I think of the state of the realm. Deign to imagine a man precipitated from the Tour Saint-Jacques. Before hitting the ground he says to himself: 'It's all right so far, but beware of the arrival!'"

"What does that allegory signify?"

"It signifies that the realm of France is falling into an abyss, at the bottom of which it will perish if it isn't saved before reaching it."

"Explain yourself."

"Everything has gone from bad to worse since your hand ceased holding the reins of the State; the prodigalities of Madame la Reine and Monseigneur le Duc d'Orléans have caused Jean Petit to say from the pulpit that they are clad in the substance of the people and only live on their tears; the right of seizure has been reestablished in spite of your ordinances; duties are forced and taxes infinitely multiplied; the charges of justices and others are sold to the highest bidder..."

"Handsome nephew," said Berry, interrupting the duc, "You're forgetting that you have just been reconciled with your cousin d'Orléans, and that you have sworn to avoid any new occasion for discord. In any case, nothing is lost. Our nephew d'Orléans is prepared to confront all the necessities by means of the levy of the annual tax."

"That tax will be the second of the year," replied Bourgogne.

"Where has the money from the first gone?" asked the king.

"It is all spent; the coffers are entirely empty," replied the queen, looking at Bourgogne with a challenging expression.

"How have they been exhausted? Have we had some ruinous war?"

"No, Sire; the war against the English is being fought from castle to castle; the seigneurs are supporting the expenses alone."

"So, Madame, all that gold has been foolishly dissipated?"

"Sire, you're offending your brother and me without justice. Everything has been consecrated to magnificent works of art, fêtes and tourneys appropriate to recreate the populace and cause them to marvel."

"Yes," replied Boulogne, brutally, "by such signs that resulted in the rebellion of the Maillotins, which shook the throne more than the English."

"Agreed," said Berry, supported by his brothers, "but what good does it do to throw stones at the past? Let's only think about providing for the future. There's a means, the recasting of the money."

"The recasting of money!" cried Jean *Sans Peur*. "You want the people of Paris running at barricades with pikes? They'll have us boiled like forgers."

"Vain words," interjected Isabeau. "It's necessary to have money at any price."

"For further prodigalities?"

"That's too much, Monsieur de Bourgogne; you're lacking respect for the king in lacking it for the queen." Isabeau made as if to get up.

"Stay here, Madame," said Charles VI. "We are united in the Council of State; it is to discuss and seek the truth, however disagreeable one of us might be. Oh, why was it necessary for me to recover my reason? The present saddens me, the future frightens me. I won't talk about the past—which is to say, my minority. That's nothing compared with what has been done during my malady. Who trusts me? What can be done?"

"There is only one remedy, Sire, "said Bourgogne, "and that is to convene the Estates General."

"The Estates General!" murmured the seigneurs of Orléans' party.

"Yes, the Estates General," affirmed Jean *Sans Peur*. He addressed the king: "That deference toward your subjects, Sire, will calm minds and will submit them to new subsidies, applicable this time only to the needs of the realm."

"The Estates General," said Berry. "What does that institution signify except the debasement of royalty? The king is only responsible to God. In difficult times he can hold counsel with his nobility, but descend any lower? Never!"

While the Armagnacs applauded and the Bourguignons did the opposite, Isabeau wondered what had become of Orléans, and ended up telling herself that he could only be retained by some gallant work.

"My cousin Bourgogne," said the king, who had collected himself, "we are grateful to you for having bravely attacked the administration of the government and finances in recent times, but be careful that the great enthusiasm you testify in favor if the populace does not give rise to the accusation of thoughts of ambition."

"Touché," murmured Berry, addressing his two brothers. Aloud, he added: "Admirably reasoned, Sire!"

"Monseigneur de Berry," retorted the king, "we shall not dissimulate from you either that we also hold in suspicion assemblies exclusively composed of peers and batons. Such an assembly would choose, to substitute for me, the prince who has always protected the nobility. Therefore, either Bourgogne or Orléans! If my brother were here I would say to him: 'I pardon you for what you have done, but I don't want you, even so, to recommence,' It's not a matter of me, it's a matter of the public good. Ah, we're no longer in the times of Charlemagne, when there were only nobles and serfs. The serfs have gradually redeemed themselves; commons have formed; the bourgeoisie has acquired freedom and wealth; it is becoming the counterweight of the nobility. It's necessary to think of establishing equilibrium. But first of all, for an initial resolution, annul the ordinance that was wrenched from me in 1406 and which attributed to my brother the supervision of finance and to the queen the presidency of the council."

"But Sire," said the queen, "I haven't merited..."

"Don't interrupt me, Madame. That is what I shall do, for my will is determined. I do not intend you to have any further part in public affairs. As for my brother, he will no longer have the opportunity to satisfy, at the expense of the State treasury, his immoderate appetite for luxury and fêtes. It is to our cousin Bourgogne that I will confide the finances. Such a change attracts to whoever holds it the hatred of the populace. I hope that his popularity will not be worn away too rapidly. As for the government of the realm, it will be shared between Bourgogne and Orléans. No ordinance will be valid unless it is signed by both of them."

"But what if there is a divergence of opinion?" asked Berry.

"In that case, the Estates are to be concerned and Orléans and Bourgogne dismissed. That, I hope, will consolidate their reconciliation. I have spoken."

He made a sign to the assembly to separate.

Isabeau de Bavière was disconcerted; the others said to one another what the chronicle has retained: "When Charles VI is not the maddest, he is the wisest man in the realm."

226

XXX. THE ANDALUSIAN[52]

"Charles VI, says an old chronicle, in his time was piteous, mild and benign to his people, serving and loving God and a great almoner. He had a colorless face and half-closed eyes. He seemed to be asleep, his head covered by a hood with a short peak, and he walked through the Hôtel Saint-Pol after holding the Council of State looking here and there at the changes made to the said house, like a man long absent remembering everything in its location and placement."

In fact, the king seemed to be recovering the possession of his reason seriously and reentering perfectly into normal life. He came and went through his house as if to rediscover it.

There was no news in Paris except of his recovery and his virile declaration in the session of the Council of State. His return to reason was celebrated in the churches and masses were said, both high and low, for his complete cure.

The queen did not blame herself for having hindered that reawakening. She sought, on the other hand, to forget the infidelities of the king's brother in the company of the Seigneur de Boisbourdon, a handsome knight whom she had attached to her person,

---

[52] Editor's note: "We have respected even the weaknesses of Gérard de Nerval's work; it is quite certain that this last chapter has remained in the state of a sketch rather than a finished work. We shall give it as we have found it, making a scruple of developing it and substituting ourselves for the author, who left his work unfinished."

In the meantime, Marguerite de Hainaut, the wife of Jean *Sans Peur*, in the costume of a young seigneur, was introduced into the Hôtel de Brehaigne at the moment when Marguerite d'Anghuien, in a similar disguise, left it in order to go in search of her son in the abode of the Prince of Fools. But Raoulet d'Actonville had come to look for him there, in order to indicate to him the surest way of extracting his mother from the hands of Orléans.

As they were heading for the Hôtel d'Artois, the house of the Duc de Bourgogne, they encountered the mendicant brother, who was still pursuing his quest through the streets. Richard approached him as one approaches a confessor, and asked him for his absolution for the mission that he had promised his father to fulfill

Jean Petit contented himself with saying to him: *Fiat voluntas Dei*, but in a tone such that Richard was terrified by it.

The poor boy was as if petrified. Raoulet d'Actonville dragged him away and, a moment later, in a house near the Porte Barbette, near the house of Maréchal d'Évreaux, not far from the Hôtel d'Artois, Eustache Maillet,[53] the water-carrier we have seen exposed in the pillory, and Richard Carpalin were sitting at table, face to face, as they had been in the pillory, recounting their emotion and their rancor.

What was the Duc d'Orléans doing in his Château de Beauté? He was under the charm of the beautiful Andalusian that Gonin had sent him, with a retinue of dancers.

Rita possessed the complex type in which one finds Moorish blood mingled with the ancient blood of Spain:

---

[53] The author has apparently forgotten that this character's forename was previously given as Nicolas.

a slightly aquiline nose, fine lips, arched and well-furnished eyebrows, glittering blue eyes shaded by long silky lashes and a mat complexion that sometimes blushed slightly. Her small and dainty figure had a rare flexibility. When she delivered herself to the dances of her native land she was ravishing, with her ebony hair, which flowed over the contour of her hips, and her splendid breasts, retained like Messalina's by a simple gold ribbon. Around her agitated the bacchantes that the Prince of Fools had collected in the Court of Miracles, whose métier was dancing in the streets with castanets until the age when they became prostitutes.

Louis abandoned himself to that prepared intoxication without thinking about anything else. The State, his brother and his enemy were all forgotten.

It was, however, necessary to think about the retreat. When the seneschal understood that the hour of lassitude had arrived he said to Jacob: "Let's go, genteel page. Go have Monseigneur's mule saddled and bridled. The trot of a horse would inconvenience him; the trot of the mule is mild and regular."

Jacob obeyed. The Duc bestrode his mount nonchalantly and traveled gently, accompanied by his page on horseback.

While they were advancing in the direction of the Château de Vincennes, Charles VI had made a virile resolution. While roaming the house he had arrived at the queen's private apartment and had surprised Boisbourdon at her knees. The suitor, in the king's order, was immediately apprehended, sewn into a sack and thrown into the Seine. As for Isabeau, similarly seized, she was taken to the Château d'Amboise, where she was to be kept prisoner while awaiting her condemnation to capital punishment or perpetual reclusion in a monastery.[54]

The king had shown an astonishing decisiveness. People wondered whether he had recovered his reason completely, or whether his mind was becoming unbalanced again.

I expected it! Bourgogne said to himself.

Suddenly, cries coming from the street made Charles VI shudder. What is it?" he asked

Savoisy, who had raced to the balcony, cried: "Monseigneur d'Orléans..." He dared not finish.

"Well, what about my brother?"

"Alas, Sire, assassinated."

"Assassinated!" repeated the king, closing into a chair, around which all the seigneurs gathered, with the exception of Bourgogne, who took advantage of the general emotion to disappear.

He said to himself: *Raoulet d'Actonville has been exact. It only remains for me to wait. The king won't recover...and I'll no longer have anything confronting me but a culpable woman whom the Parlement won't fail to strike.*

With that, Jean *Sans Peur* went through a hidden door and returned rapidly to his house. He chose the most ardent of his horses, and, accompanied by devoted servants, departed at top speed for Saint-Maxent, had the

---

[54] This is fictitious; Isabeau left Paris after the assassination of Orléans in order to attempt to organize opposition to the Burgundians in the name of her son, the dauphin. The resultant civil war dragged on until 1419, when Jean *Sans Peur* was assassinated, after apparently being lured into a trap by the dauphin.

bridge there broken behind him and went to establish himself in Reims, his quarter of observation.

Scarcely had he emerged from the Hôtel de Saint-Pol than a stretcher went in, on which the Duc d'Orléans was lying. He had not only been stabbed, but his right hand had been severed. In his left arm he was clutching Jacob's cadaver to his breast.

Raoulet d'Actonville had gone to rejoin his master, carrying that severed hand, which he threw at the Duc's feet, singing:

... one evening my straying hand
Undid her gilded belt
And loosened her blonde hair.

When the stretcher was brought into the room where the king was, the latter, who had lost consciousness at the news of the murder, had not come round

A large number of the inhabitants of the Rue Vieille-du-Temple, behind which Jean Petit and Gonin were, formed a procession for the dead and the dying. The man-at-arms Riblet followed, holding Richard Carpalin by the collar, who was searching with his gaze for Bourgogne, in order to recommend himself to him.

"Here's one of the assassins," said Riblet.

The Duc d'Orléans raised a last gaze upon the murder and murmured: "My son! The son of Mariette d'Anghuien; and the poor child here"—he made an effort to place his lips on Jacob's—"is also my son, that of Coline Demerre. Richard, you have killed your father and your brother."

Then the Duc let his head fall back; he was dead.

"Is that true?" stammered Richard, wildly.

"It's true," replied Gonin.

"It's true," added Jean Petit.

"Oh, wretch that I am!" sighed Richard.

Disengaging himself rapidly from Riblet's grip he ran to the balcony and leapt over it with one bound. A dull sound was heard; Richard had fallen on to his mother, who was returning from Gonin's lair, and had killed her.

Jean Petit took the arm of the Prince of Fools and drew him into a corner of the room, after having pushed back his hood.

"Do you recognize me today?" A ferocious joy illuminated the grim face, which Gonin recognized immediately.

"Aubert Le Flamenc!" he murmured, fearfully.

"In religion, Jean Petit."

The king only recovered his senses late in the night. He conserved enough reason to order the arrest of Jean de Bourgogne, who could not be arrested.

Later, the madness of the king, the return of the murderer and Isabeau de Bavière, and the apologies for the murder by Jean Petit, had the murder considered as a deliverance for virtue.

Marguerite de Hainaut retired to the duchy of Bourgogne, where her rude husband, believing her to have been calumniated, left her in peace. Jean Petit remained in history as a terrible orator.

As for the Prince of Fools, if he was a precursor of Molière in comedy, he also was in death; he died, like him, on stage, playing his favorite role of Satan.

ALSO FROM BLACK COAT PRESS

( ) Marie Catherine d'Aulnoy. Tales of the Fays 1
( ) Marie Catherine d'Aulnoy. Tales of the Fays 2
( ) Honoré de Balzac. The Last Fay
( ) Mme Barbot de Villeneuve. The Naiads * Beauty and the Beast
( ) Cyprien Bérard. The Vampire Lord Ruthwen
( ) S. Henry Berthoud. The Angel Asrael
( ) Aloysius Bertrand. Gaspard de la Nuit
( ) Charlotte-Rose Caumont de La Force. The Land of Delights
( ) Comte de Caylus. The Impossible Enchantment
( ) Félicien Champsaur. Pharaoh's Wife
( ) Comtesse D.L. The Tyranny of the Fays Abolished
( ) Alexandre Dumas (w/Paul Lacroix). The Man who Married a Mermaid
( ) Marie-Antoinette Fagnan. The Enchanter's Mirror
( ) Paul Féval. Anne of the Isles
( ) Paul Féval. Bel Demonio
( ) Paul Féval. The Black Coats: The Cadet Gang
( ) Paul Féval. The Black Coats: The Companions of the Treasure
( ) Paul Féval. The Black Coats: Heart of Steel
( ) Paul Féval. The Black Coats: The Invisible Weapon
( ) Paul Féval. The Black Coats: The Parisian Jungle
( ) Paul Féval. The Black Coats: 'Salem Street
( ) Paul Féval. The Black Coats: The Sword Swallower
( ) Paul Féval: The Companions of the Silence
( ) Paul Féval: John Devil
( ) Paul Féval: Knightshade
( ) Paul Féval: Revenants
( ) Paul Féval: Vampire City
( ) Paul Féval. The Vampire Countess

233

( ) Paul Féval. The Wandering Jew's Daughter
( ) Charles de Fieux, Chevalier de Mouhy. Lamekis
( ) Judith Gautier: Isoline and the Serpent-Flower
( ) Jules Janin. The Magnetized Corpse
( ) Gustave Kahn. The Tale of Gold and Silence
( ) Paul Lacroix. Danse Macabre
( ) Louis-Guillaume de La Follie. The Unpretentious Philoso-pher
( ) Etienne-Léon de Lamothe-Langon. The Virgin Vampire
( ) Etienne-Léon de Lamothe-Langon. The Mysterious Hermit of the Tomb
( ) Maurice Level. The Gates of Hell
( ) Marie-Jeanne L'Héritier de Villandon. The Robe of Sincer-ity
( ) André Lichtenberger. The Centaurs
( ) André Lichtenberger. The Children of the Crab
( ) Monsieur de Listonai. The Philosophical Voyager
( ) Jean-Marc & Randy Lofficier. The French Fantasy Treas-ury (Vol. 1) (anthology)
( ) Jean-Marc & Randy Lofficier. The French Fantasy Treas-ury (Vol. 2) (anthology)
( ) Jean-Marc & Randy Lofficier. The French Fantasy Treas-ury (Vol. 3) (anthology)
( ) Charles Lomon & P.-B. Gheusi. The Last Days of Atlantis
( ) Marie-Madeleine de Lubert. Princess Camion
( ) Charles Malato. Lost!
( ) Maurice Magre. The Marvelous Story of Claire d'Amour
( ) Maurice Magre. The Call of the Beast
( ) Maurice Magre. Priscilla of Alexandria
( ) Maurice Magre. The Angel of Lust
( ) Maurice Magre. The Mystery of the Tiger
( ) Maurice Magre. The Poison of Goa
( ) Maurice Magre. Lucifer
( ) Maurice Magre. The Blood of Toulouse
( ) Maurice Magre. The Albigensian Treasure
( ) Maurice Magre. Jean de Fodoas
( ) Maurice Magre. Melusine

( ) Maurice Magre. The Brothers of the Virgin Gold
( ) Catulle Mendes. The Little Fays in the Air
( ) Louis-Sébastien Mercier. The Iron Man
( ) Joseph Méry. The Tower of Destiny
( ) Hippolyte Mettais. Paris Before the Deluge
( ) Henriette-Julie de Murat. The Palace of Vengeance
( ) Marie Nizet. Captain Vampire
( ) Charles Nodier. Trilby * The Crumb Fairy
( ) Pierre-Alexis Ponson du Terrail. The Vampire and the Devil's Son
( ) Pierre-Alexis Ponson du Terrail. The Immortal Woman
( ) Pierre-Alexis Ponson du Terrail. The Police Agent
( ) Edgar Quinet. Ahasuerus
( ) Edgar Quinet. The Enchanter Merlin
( ) Restif de la Bretonne. Discovery of the Austral Continent
( ) Restif de la Bretonne. Posthumous Correspondence (Vol. 1)
( ) Restif de la Bretonne. Posthumous Correspondence (Vol. 2)
( ) Restif de la Bretonne. Posthumous Correspondence (Vol. 3)
( ) Restif de la Bretonne. Posthumous Correspondence (all 3 volumes)
( ) Restif de la Bretonne. The Story of the Great Prince Oribeau (The Fay Ouroucoucou 1)
( ) Restif de la Bretonne. The Four Beauties and the Four Beasts (The Fay Ouroucoucou 2)
( ) Marie-Anne de Roumier-Robert. The Voyages of Lord Seaton to the Seven Planets
( ) Louis-Claude de Saint-Martin. The Crocodile
( ) Nicolas Segur. The Human Paradise
( ) Nicolas Segur. Penelope's Secret
( ) Pierre de Sélènes. An Unknown World
( ) Brian Stableford. News from the Moon (anthology)
( ) Brian Stableford. The Germans on Venus (anthology)
( ) Brian Stableford. The Supreme Progress (anthology)
( ) Brian Stableford. The World Above the World (anthology)
( ) Brian Stableford. Nemoville (anthology)
( ) Brian Stableford. Investigations of the Future (anthology)
( ) Brian Stableford. The Conqueror of Death (anthology)

( ) Brian Stableford. The Revolt of the Machines (anthology)
( ) Brian Stableford. The Man With the Blue Face (anthology)
( ) Brian Stableford. The Aerial Valley (anthology)
( ) Brian Stableford. The New Moon (anthology)
( ) Brian Stableford. The Nickel Man (anthology)
( ) Brian Stableford. On the Brink of the Worl's End (anthology)
( ) Brian Stableford. The Mirror of Present Events (anthology)
( ) Brian Stableford. The Humanisphere (anthology)
( ) Brian Stableford. Journey to the Isles of Atlantis (anthology)
( ) Brian Stableford. The Queen of the Fays (anthology)
( ) Brian Stableford. Funestine (anthology)
( ) Brian Stableford. The Origin of the Fays (anthology)
( ) Brian Stableford. Tales of Enchantment and Disenchantment (anthology + non-fiction)
( ) Charles-François Tiphaigne de La Roche. Amilec
( ) Simon Tyssot de Patot. The Strange Voyages of Jacques Massé and Pierre de Mésange
( ) Louis Ulbach. Prince Bonifacio
( ) Villiers de l'Isle-Adam. The Scaffold
( ) Villiers de l'Isle-Adam. The Vampire Soul
( ) Willy. Astral Amour

stage plays

( ) Alevy, Marcel Nadaud, Gaston Leroux. Chéri-Bibi
( ) Anicet-Bourgeois / Lucien Dabril. Rocambole
( ) Alexandre Bisson & Guillaume Livet. Nick Carter vs. Fantômas
( ) Victor Darlay & Henry de Gorsse. Arsène Lupin vs. Sherlock Holmes
( ) Jules Dornay. Lord Ruthven Begins
( ) Alexandre Dumas. The Return of Lord Ruthven
( ) Paul Féval. Captain Phantom / Gentlemen of the Night
( ) Gaston Marot. Louis Pericaud. Sherlock Holmes vs. Jack the Ripper

( ) Charles Nodier, Antoine Beraud & Toussaint-Merle / Victor Hugo, Paul Foucher & Paul Meurice. Frankenstein / The Hunchback of Notre-Dame

( ) Charles Nodier, Eugène Scribe, J.W. Polidori. Lord Ruthven the Vampire

( ) Pierre de Wattyne & Yorril Walter. Sherlock Holmes vs. Fantômas